Kissing Mr. Mistletoe

Kate Kisset

Coming Soon from Kate Kisset:

The ladies of Bella Villa and Napa Valley's Santino brothers return in 2017 in the second book of the Single Girls Wine Club series, *Napa Crush*.

NAPA CRUSH
*Book #2: The Single Girls Wine Club
*Danica's Story

Visit Kate's website at: http://www.katekisset.com

Copyright

This book is a work of fiction. References to wines, products, real people, events, establishments, wineries, organizations or locales are intended only to provide a sense of authenticity and are used fictitiously. All other characters, incidents and dialogue are drawn from the author's imagination and are not to be construed as real.

FIRST EDITION

ISBN 978-0-9965638-6-4

EPUB EDITION NOVEMBER 2016

Formatting: Brenda Wright, Formatting Done Wright

Dedication

For everyone who believes in the power of a kiss.

Contents

You are cordially invited to spend your HOLIDAYS IN THE VINEYARD.

Ever since his last remaining relative died, country music star Trace Montgomery has avoided California, specifically his home town of Napa Valley. Trace can't stand the memories. But seven days before the holiday, he's forced to return to wine country to sell the St. Helena Christmas tree farm he inherited from his uncle. With his sidekick guitar Lola nearby, a past love falls into his arms while trying to turn a vineyard bunny sculpture into a reindeer. Now Trace can't stop thinking about her. He's making up naughty lyrics to Christmas songs.

Single mom, Monique Jacobson doesn't have time for a bath, never mind a romance. She's working hard to secure a promotion and pay raise from Santino Winery that will allow her and her daughter to move out of Nana's little B&B.

St. Helena and Napa Valley hotels are booked for the holiday, and Monique finds Trace holed up with her and her daughter at her gran's Napa B&B for a Christmas in wine country. Will they rediscover the love they lost and rekindle Christmas magic under the mistletoe?

Special note to fans of Kate Kisset's *Single Girls Wine Club* Wine Country Romance series: The ladies of Bella Villa and Napa Valley's Santino brothers return in 2017 in the second book of the series, *Napa Crush.*

Kissing Mr. Mistletoe is a standalone read. Although you may recognize some of the names, this Christmas gem features its own cast of loveable and sexy characters.

Kissing Mr. Mistletoe

Chapter 1

Monique Jacobson climbed another step above the rows of Santino cabernet vineyards. She reached out as far as she could without losing grip of the ladder. Stretching another half inch, her fingertips almost touched Bunny Fru Fru's gleaming metal nose. Frustrated, she loudly exhaled a breath of air.

After allowing only thirty-five minutes of her packed schedule to turn the massive bunny sculpture into Rudolf for the party, Monique spent fifteen minutes she didn't have finding a ladder. Then, she'd used another twenty finding someone to help her drag the clunky sixteen-footer to the vineyard and situate it under the landmark. Panic started to set in. The annual Santino Winery holiday party that Monique was in charge of for the first time started in six hours.

"Is he *ever* going to turn into Rudolf, Mommy?" Adele's voice chirped from below. With her pink cheeks glowing and surrounded by grapevines shimmering in the sun, her daughter looked like a wine country cherub. "Of course he will. Bunny Fru Fru always turns into Rudolf at Christmas. We can do anything we set our minds to, baby. Just you watch."

Spotting the red plastic nose parked in a pile of brown grape leaves at the base of a vine behind Adele, Monique turned away, cursing herself under her breath. Why didn't she take the schnozzle *with* her up the ladder?

"See it honey?" Hanging on to the ladder tight enough to lose circulation in her left hand, she cautiously lifted her right, and pointed to the shiny red object. It looked like a deflated soccer ball. "It's behind you."

Adele scrunched her nose and circled. Perusing around her feet, she then lifted her head. Her eyes became huge and she took off running. "I see it."

"Good job." Monique encouraged her without daring to change her grip. "Now hold on to it, and come closer."

Adele sucked in a deep breath, appearing to gather enough steam to make a beeline to the ladder. Monique yelled, "No running. Don't come too close sweetheart."

Standing still and clutching her prize, Adele craned her neck all the way back and squinted. "How many giant steps should I take?"

"Five, honey." Monique held on to the ladder. "I think five big-girl steps will do it."

Adele lifted her right leg and dramatically plunked

it down on the dirt two feet in front of her and then brought her left leg up. “One,” she announced, touching down and repeating the process. “Two!”

Monique hadn’t intended to take Adele to work with her, but had forgotten all about the preschool teacher holiday she’d circled on her calendar months ago. With her favorite sitter booked, she wasn’t about to leave Adele with anyone she hadn’t thoroughly investigated. Thankfully her idea of turning a day of decorating the winery into a holiday outing with Adele seemed to be working.

“Three!” Adele shrieked.

A loud sputtering engine and blaring music caused Monique to turn in time to see the Napa Pines and Wines jalopy come down the driveway. From the elevated vantage point, she saw the tree she needed for the tasting room in the bed of the truck. Heaving a sigh of relief, she rotated back to Adele.

“Four, Mommy! I’m getting close. . .” Adele took another step. “Five!”

“Perfect honey. Now stay right where you are and remember to never, ever, climb a ladder like this without my help.”

“And Daddy's?” Adele asked, cradling the red nose.

Her heart sank, knowing her former husband Jarod would never help his daughter with a ladder or anything else. Why must Adele always ask about that deadbeat? Time after time Monique covered for Jarod's negligence, hating to see Adele's hopes smashed. They always were. Jarod never showed up, kept any of his promises, or followed through with anything except getting her pregnant. The privilege and joy of being Adele's mother made up for all of her disappointment, but it didn't ease any of her daughter's pain.

"Yes, and Daddy's help too." Monique's stomach roiled looking at Adele's innocent expression. Maybe this year, he'd finally see her for Christmas.

"Do you think you can throw Rudolf's nose up to me so we can turn this bunny into a reindeer?" Monique carefully let go of the ladder with her right hand and leaned, stretching it out to Adele. "Throw it now, honey." She held her breath.

Adele didn't wait for further instruction and hurled the plastic nose into the air. Spinning, the snout missed Monique's outstretched hand and continued its path of projection several feet over her head and to the right.

Rudolf's schnozzle caught the light and sparkling in the sun, made its descent. Monique shifted her weight to grab it. *Almost there.* She reached up and over feeling the ladder sway and rock beneath her.

"Mommy!"

Quickly seizing her perch with both hands, the sole of her boot slipped sideways on the metal step. Instead of regaining her balance, Monique skidded down one rung, and then another with her left foot and then another and another, until she found herself rappelling backward down the ladder, desperately grappling to hang on to whatever she could and praying for a soft landing.

"Mommy!"

She missed the last step and hit the ground, landing flat on her back.

"Oh no!" Adele scampered to her and laid her soft chubby hands on Monique's cheeks. Snuggling close, her sweet breath touched her skin. Adele inspected her eyes from an inch away. "Are you hurt bad?"

"I'm okay, baby." Reaching behind her back, Monique found the rock digging into her spine. She plucked it out of the dirt and flung it.

"You shouldn't be climbing on top of something you can't handle."

Every cell of Monique's body froze. Her heart paused mid-thump. The familiar drawl of the deep, sexy, voice coming from above propelled her back in time at warp speed to six years ago. But it couldn't be him. Not in a million years. She wrapped one arm tightly around Adele, and shielding her eyes from the glare with the other, looked up. *Shit.*

Trace Montgomery towered over her. He folded his arms over his chest making his smooth, muscled biceps bulge under his navy T-shirt. Wearing jeans that fit him as precisely as a fireman carries a hose, and with his swagger apparently still intact, he leaned back on the heel of his boot and tilted his face, rubbing his jaw. His unmistakable green eyes sparkled down at her.

"W-what are you doing here?"

"You're hardly in a position to be asking questions." Trace reached with a powerful hand and lifted her and Adele to their feet.

After removing a twig wedged between her legs and butt cheek, Monique attempted to get her bearings. Her brain stuttered, stopped and skipped over the right words to say. Her libido, however, operated flawlessly. Tingles charged from her neck to her toes and she broke into a sweat. Steadying her gaze on his preposterously handsome face, a result of mixed genctic magic, her heart beat out of her chest. Trace opened his arms for a hug. Before she could think, he wrapped them around her and squeezed, smelling like—well, smelling like Trace, a combination of clean, fresh and *help me now, Jesus.*

Releasing her from the embrace, he took hold of her hands, and gently swung them. "My God, it's good to see you again, Monique."

"W-what—I thought you were on the road—with your band?" Suddenly remembering Adele, Monique pulled her close to her hip.

A dimple flashed next to his devilish grin as Trace reached for her face. The world skidded into slow-motion. Monique held her breath, watching his bicep flex and his hand move closer and closer to her ear. "So you've been checking up on me? Brushing her skin with his fingers, he pulled a crispy grape leaf out of her hair and then stepped back. "I'm flattered."

"I asked Joe Rozzi at the Christmas tree farm how you were doing when I ordered the tree." Monique winced. She inquired about Trace whenever she had the opportunity but didn't necessarily want him to be aware of her snooping. "I'm not one of your crazy fans—if that's what you're worried about."

She could find him anywhere and had DVR'ed his *Kimmel* appearance three days ago. Even though they'd only dated for six months, a man like Trace Montgomery would leave an indelible impression on any woman.

Only three feet away from his twinkling green eyes, she averted her gaze, trying not to remember the private songs he used to sing to her, how safe she felt wrapped in his arms, or the way he tasted. . . *No. Let's not go there.*

What would her life be like now if she had joined

him on tour when he'd asked? *It's all in the past.* Adele came into her world and nothing else mattered.

"Tour's over," he grinned, checking her out, not seeming to mind when she caught him. "Maybe we'll have some time to get together? I'm only back for a week." His voice sank. "I'm finally settling my uncle's estate. Wish I had sold the place right after he died."

"Oh." She should've called, but didn't have the strength to not run back into his life. After the release of his number one hit, "Love me Like Crazy," Trace should've been celebrating. Instead, he'd suffered more heartache than anyone she knew. Both of his parents had died in a head-on, less than a mile from here. And last year, he lost his uncle Glenn. "I'm very sorry for your loss Trace. I should've reached out."

He ran his boot over some loose dirt. "Thank you. I appreciate it." Rubbing his bottom lip, he brought his focus back to her. "You look good enough to. . ." His mouth curved up and he laid a devilish smirk on her boots. From her ankles, he eyed her legs, then his gaze traveled slowly up her thighs and paused at her hips.

Putting a stop to his strip search by stare, Monique crossed her arms before his eyes got to her chest. Unfortunately, the move had the opposite effect and lifted her breasts out over her arms.

His eyebrows shot to his forehead, with a question. "You look fantastic by the way." Monique caught her mouth hanging open and clamped it shut, but couldn't stop beaming.

Forgetting mommy duties for a second, she flipped back in time to her former flirtatious self. Caught in his snare, she blurted, "You're looking pretty hot there yourself—cowboy." Saying it out loud brought her back to earth. Trace wrangled women, not steers, and wondering what on earth possessed her to call *him of all people* hot, she wanted to take the words back. She didn't have time for flirting. She rarely had time for a bath. Monique brushed the dirt off her butt. "I'm sorry if I'm so—I'm—Joe mentioned you were coming out to visit the farm, I just didn't expect to see you"—she waved a hand over the vineyards—"here."

Smiling, Trace ran a hand through his light brown hair "I arrived a few hours ago. Didn't expect to play Santa delivering trees, but Joe's daughter is having a baby so I'm covering."

"Jessica went into labor today?"

"Mama." Adele tugged on her shirt. "Is he the man we saw on TV?" Trace cocked his head.

"You were watching me, huh?"

The last thing Trace needed was encouragement. He'd take an inch and she'd end up buck naked with her boots on the dashboard of that old Christmas tree truck. Buying time, Monique tugged on a vine and wound it around her finger, trying to think of a fib to worm her way out of being caught fawning over his recent television special. She couldn't come up with any lie Adele wouldn't catch her on.

"I don't believe we've met." Trace crouched down to Adele's eye level. "What's your name?"

"I'm Adele Jacobson." She jutted her hand out for a shake. "And I'm four." He clutched her tiny fingers in his big hand.

"*Jacobson* . . . Well, I'll be, Trace said glancing up at Monique. Then he aimed his charm back on her daughter. "Adele Jacobson, what a lovely name, and you have your mother's exceptional blue eyes too, don't you? Call me Trace."

As he straightened, Adele craned her neck back, keeping eye contact all the way up. "We were trying to make Bunny Fru Fru—Rudolph." Adele pouted her plump lips and pointed to the limp nose stuck between two vines, hanging on a wire.

Trace followed the direction of her finger and casually strolled over to the cable. "This is what turns a flying rabbit into a reindeer?" After untangling the plastic snout, he waved it at Adele.

"Uh huh." Adele nodded. "But p-please be careful. Mommy says it's not a toy." Trace tossed his head back, laughing, unleashing the wide insanely wonderful smile Monique hadn't seen in person for so long. It lit up his face and made the sun seem brighter.

"I promise to be careful." Standing in front of a row of yellow and red vines, Trace furrowed his brows, scrutinizing the airless ball and stuck his hand into the slit destined for the bunny's muzzle. Hanging on to it, he ambled to the ladder.

"No." Monique trailed him. "We don't need any help. We've got this."

He swiveled his neck around and shot her a smirk, then gripped the ladder and began climbing.

"You really don't have to do that," she tried again.

With his blue jeans hugging and flashing boot leather under the hem, up, up, the ladder he climbed.

"Careful, it isn't steady," Monique said, grabbing Adele's hand.

Trace threw her a grin, but Monique barely noticed because she wasn't eyeing his face. His butt looked stupendous up there.

"Please don't hurt yourself." She held her breath.

"It's kind of"—Trace reached the top— "tricky."

Without another glance down, Trace leaned over, and secured the red ball onto Bunny Fru Fru's nose. After effortlessly descending from the ladder, he tossed his hair back and with extra bluster in his step, strolled over.

"Rudolph!" Adele broke into a smile wider than her little hand could cover. "Mommy, it's Rudolph!" She giggled, pointing at the reindeer in all of his gleaming magnificence.

Monique caught his eye. “Thank you, Trace.”

“Don’t mention it.” He winked.

Gulp.

“Thank you, Mr. Trace, for helping Rudolf.”

“Happy to assist, Miss Adele.” He adjusted the fabric at his knees and crouched down. Monique tried to recall the last time a man Adele’s father’s age had given her the time of day. “It just wouldn’t be Christmas without big bunny Rudolf guiding Santa into the valley, right?”

“Right!” She shot up her hand, and he clapped it. “High five!”

“So.” Getting out of his crouch, Trace brushed his hands together. “Are you ladies ready to see your masterpiece?”

“You have no idea how much I’m counting on this tree.” She grabbed Adele’s hand. “Almost time for decorating.” When her boss, Michael Santino, surprised her in October by assigning her the responsibility of the Santino Winery holiday party, Monique jumped into action. Although Michael, the eldest of six Santino brothers, ran Napa’s prestigious Santino Corporation with his father, the winery was Michael’s baby. All of their worldwide businesses stemmed from the success of Napa Valley’s Santino wines. The entire Santino family and their closest friends would attend the party and if there was one family you didn't want to disappoint it was the Santinos, especially at Christmas.

After hiring a designer to create custom wine bottle ornaments featuring miniature Santino wine labels, Monique ordered a specifically sized tree to show them off. If she impressed Michael with the party tonight, maybe she'd finally get a promotion. She hated denying Adele the new clothes she needed or the kitty backpack and playhouse she wanted. If she could just get a raise, Monique could climb out of the financial hole Jarod had left her in.

"Right this way, ladies," Trace said, grinning. When they reached the truck, he threw his head back. "Let the jingle bells ring." Resting his arm on the side of the vehicle, he waved them over. "Come on. Get a load of this beauty."

After waiting months for this moment, Monique could barely contain her excitement. Clutching its cool metal side, she peered into the truck, and her heart hit the dirt. "That's not the tree."

Trace frowned. He glanced into the bed and back at her. "Of course it is."

Tears welling in her eyes, Monique blinked them back. *No raise.* Why had she put her faith in Joe Rozzi at the Christmas tree lot? Joe guaranteed he'd have her tree delivered by today, and now her party plans were ruined. The whole shebang hitched on the custom adornments, now waiting in boxes, ready to be hung on a particular sized tree. She didn't have time to track down another one before the party. "No. It's not what I ordered."

The corners of Trace's lips drooped, something that rarely happened. "Yes, it is. When Joe told me I'd be delivering it to you, I even double-checked the paperwork. I remember how picky you can be."

"Well." She sighed. "I ordered a twelve-foot blue spruce with enough space between the branches for specific ornaments, and that appears to be a scrawny Leyland cypress."

"Like the Charlie Brown tree?" Adele asked.

"Yes, sweetheart, exactly like the Charlie Brown tree." She redirected her focus from Adele to Trace, narrowing her eyes. "And although the puny pine was pretty in its *make-believe* way," she said raising her eyebrows, "I *have* to have a *particular* tree for my plans to *work*." Her ears thudded, waiting for his response.

"It's okay, Mommy, maybe he's only good at singing." Adele scampered off a few yards and found a stick.

Trace crossed his arms in front of him and harrumphed in a way that made his pecs bulge. "You need to take another look."

Acknowledging his frustration, and trying not to be too distracted by his annoyingly masculine physique, Monique angled her chin down and inspected the truck's bed again.

"Now, see? It's a fine tree. Once you get your hands on it and cover it with lights, you'll be all set."

"No." She shook her head. "I can tell you right now, we shouldn't bother moving it into the winery because it's a waste of time." She studied his dumbfounded expression. "It isn't going to work."

Although he used to be perceptive when they dated, Trace threw her a blank stare, seeming to not understand she wasn't a magician, didn't have a magic wand and therefore couldn't do anything with that measly tree to merit a promotion.

"Look." She pressed against the truck on her tiptoes, dipped into the bed and grabbed a damp branch. Fresh sap stuck to her palm. Trace touched the back of her shoulder, completely invading her personal space, and leaned against her backside presumably to get a better look. The intoxicating scent of leather and sexy-man coming off of him, combined with the smell of fresh-cut pine made her dizzy. She gulped a deep breath, and concentrated on the task at hand, her career and Adele's future.

"There are only a few inches, at most, between the branches." She wedged her hand in between the pointed needles and grasped the tree trunk. "See? There isn't any place for me to hang the bottle ornaments. They'll get squished, and if I start cutting branches, there won't be any tree left."

She let go of the trunk. The fresh boughs bounced back in place. "I don't know what to do at this point," she muttered, stepping away from Trace and the jalopy. Throwing her hands in the air like an Italian, even though she wasn't one, she moaned. "I'm only making a big deal out of this because I'm trying to get a promotion."

She glanced at Adele drawing in the dirt and something clicked. The sight of her cheerfully absorbed in the simple beauty of her art project gave Monique a chance to refocus on what really mattered.

"I'm sorry I blew a gasket. No one is dying here." She sighed. "I'm running the party tonight, and wanted it to be perfect." Unfortunately, her eyes began to well again and her chin started quivering. She inspected a clump of dry pine needles on the ground so Trace wouldn't notice she'd become an emotional wreck over the last six years.

"I'll tell you what." Trace pulled keys out of his pocket. "Your tree is probably still in the lot with a delivery tag. I'll jet back and get it." Monique caught the familiar glint under his black lashes.

God, how she loved the way Trace used to make

her feel like the most beautiful woman on the planet.

"Hey, to be honest, I don't know the difference between a spruce, a General Lee, or what kind of tree Charlie Brown had for that matter. With Joe so worried about Jessica having a baby, who knows? Maybe I brought the wrong one."

"Oh my God. Do you think it's still at Napa Pines?"

Trace shrugged. "It's worth a try."

"Thank you. Thank you. I'll go to the lot with you, though, just to be sure it's the right one. Okay?" She pivoted to Adele. "Honey, have you finished your drawing?"

"Almost, Mommy." Adele added a circle to her picture and after tossing her stick, galloped back to her.

Trace took long, sexy strides to the passenger side of the truck and gallantly opened the door.

"Oh, no." She took Adele's hand. There was absolutely no chance in hell she'd risk having her female body parts encased in a vehicle with that tall drink of . . . sexy songwriter. In a drought for so long, Monique didn't trust her nipples or anything tingling below to behave. Trace already wreaked enough havoc on her breasts and he'd barely touched her. Suddenly springing out of a long dormancy, Monique kept having to hide her high beams with her arms. "We'll take our car."

He squinted at her. "You can drive with me, Monique."

"No. I can do this by myself. Adele and I don't need any help. Besides, I don't want you to have to drag us around and interrupt your day." She folded her arms over her chest, smashing her breasts against her body.

Trace brought his hand to his face and massaged his chin. "After six years, I finally see you again, and after only ten minutes, you're already being stubborn."

She jutted her chin out, returning his grumpy grimace right over her nose.

"We're going to the *same* place, Monique." He shifted his weight from one boot to the other and cocked his head. His sultry green gaze, the same one that transformed his fans into quivering bowls of pudding, scanned her body like an X-ray and then locked on her eyes. "I have the only truck on the lot. Therefore, *I* will be driving said truck back to this very location, with the right tree, hopefully."

"Well, okay then," she mumbled. Adele would sit in the middle as a blockade between any bumping thighs or arms. "I just didn't want to put you out."

He opened the door. "Please get in."

Chapter 2

Trace Montgomery would've recognized Monique's curves anywhere, but to have them literally drop out of the sky from a ladder shocked him senseless. He still couldn't comprehend the presence of the small girl smelling like strawberries and mud sitting beside him.

Although known for his creative prowess, Trace prided himself on his ability to keep his head on straight, but not today. The image of his past love with the clear, blue December sky backlighting her perfect butt in those jeans while she leaned over that bunny, would be etched in his memory forever.

He turned the ignition key and thought his body would combust. The demo track of "But I Love You More" blasted from the truck's speakers. Adele squealed, covering her ears.

"Hey, it's not terrible." Chuckling from nerves mostly, Trace popped the disk out of the stereo. And just in case Monique and her offspring were a hallucination, did a double take when he shoved the disk into the CD case. As sure as his guitar-picking fingers were on the wheel, Monique and her daughter were in the truck with him.

Side by side, with Adele strapped between him and Monique, they bounced over the potholes of the vineyard until the tires hit the smooth main road of Santino Winery. *How on earth did Jarod Jacobson manage to con Monique into marrying him?*

"Thanks for doing this." Monique's smile hit him from across the seat.

"You're welcome." He stole another glance from the corner of his eye. With her skin practically glowing, and the sun streaming through the window making her long, honey colored hair sparkle, the one that got away still looked like an angel. His chest tightened.

"So, Jarod Jacobson, huh?" He had examined Monique's left hand close-up when she grabbed the tree trunk, and didn't notice a ring.

"He's my daddy!"

"Yes, he is, honey." Monique leaned around Adele. "Jarod and I got divorced two years ago."

"I'm sorry to hear it." Trace couldn't imagine what kind of drama Jarod put her through and opted not to ask about the likely sordid details in front of Adele.

"So what are the plans for your trip?" Monique asked, shuffling in the seat. "Any wine tasting? The new Santino Zin won Best in Show Red in San Francisco last week."

Trace's Uncle Glenn had delivered Christmas trees to all of the wineries in the valley for as long as he could remember. The entire Santino clan attended the funeral last year. Trace hoped to have the chance to tell them how much it meant to have them there.

"I don't know if I'll have time to stop by any wineries or do much visiting this trip. I need to find an accountant." *Accounting? Really? That's the best you can do with Monique?*

Trace stole another glance at the gorgeous creature sitting three feet away. He'd never met anyone with eyes the same color, except for Adele five minutes ago. "I need someone to give me the bottom line on the tree farm's financials. I should call Michael, I'll bet he has a name. Then I need to track down a real estate agent."

After waiting thirteen months to deal with his inheritance, Trace wanted to put it, and all the memories of death and sadness, behind him—the sooner the better. Although his Uncle Glenn's generosity touched him, he didn't need the money and had no interest in growing Christmas trees for a living.

He navigated onto Route 29 heading toward Calistoga, and a crushing feeling from years ago came back. As he approached the patch of road where his parents had died, he rolled his shoulders, trying to ease the tension. *They're all gone.*

"Well, you sure have hit the big leagues since the

last time we saw each other. Congratulations, Trace. I knew you'd make it."

Silently, he thanked Monique for getting his head out of the dark place it was heading. Twinkle lights flickering around festive storefront windows caused him to slow the truck. Candy canes and toy soldiers decorated the sidewalks of downtown St. Helena. Passing the old Camelia Theatre, Trace stopped for a group of distracted shoppers loaded with bags that were cutting across Main Street.

Although he and his folks lived in Napa, Trace and his family spent most weekends between Thanksgiving and Christmas helping his aunt and uncle at their Christmas tree farm right outside St. Helena on the way to Calistoga. Martini's Pub, the old Freshee Freeze, Modela's Bakery, the pharmacy, every shop he passed, looked exactly the same. The town hadn't changed, but he had. Trace tried not to think of all the times he'd spent with his family here.

Adele started wriggling and poked him with her elbow. "Look, Mommy!"

He checked the rearview and leaned on the brakes to give Adele a better view.

"Santa." She leaned over Monique pointing out the passenger window. "And one, two, three—nine reindeer. There's Rudolph!"

Trace grinned.

Monique craned her neck around Adele. "They put up the community Christmas display a few weeks ago."

"Sorry I missed the party."

Further up the highway, The Napa Pines and Wines Christmas Tree Farm sign came into view, and Trace pulled into the rocky driveway. After parking, they clamored out of the noisy old heap. Adele tore off to the lot's gift shop, and he and Monique hurried to catch up with her. Smells of earth and fresh rain permeated the rickety shack.

"No baby today. Poor Jessica. She had those fake labor pains. Braxton Hicks," Joe Rozzi announced, handing Adele a candy cane.

Louis Armstrong's "Zat You, Santa Claus?" played over tinny speakers. As far back as Trace could remember, Joe had been his uncle's right-hand man. During the off-season, he planted the trees, and the day after Thanksgiving, he'd help open the Christmas tree lot. The tradition had come to an end last year. At Trace's request, Joe took over all of the responsibilities of the farm after his uncle passed away.

"Hello, Joe." Monique lifted her hand waving her fingers. When he dashed around the counter and greeted her with a bear hug, Trace had to admit he felt a little jealous. "Are you relieved about the false alarm or still worried about Jessica going into labor?"

"I'm on pins and needles, pardon the pun. It took Barb and me so long to have a child, I never imagined I'd still be around to meet my grandbaby. I'm thrilled. Scared. I don't know what to think." He put his hands on his hips. "What did you think of the tree, huh? Here to get another?"

"Well." Monique drew a line through sawdust on the counter with her finger.

"I hope it's still here . . ." Trace stuck his hands in his pockets. "I delivered the wrong one."

"Nah. I haven't sold any twelve-foot blue spruces today." Joe dismissed him with his hand. "It's got to be around the back."

Monique clutched Adele's hand and they followed Joe out of the building. Something about the sight of Adele holding her candy cane and grinning up at her mom with pure adoration tugged at Trace's heart. He stayed behind, not wanting to interrupt, or ruin their moment. Sure, he'd sold his share of records and launched a pretty successful music career, but over the last six years, Monique had created a family.

"Here it is." Joe pointed to a massive heap on the ground. "Got to go, customers are waiting. But that's the one you're looking for," Joe said before leaving.

Even with its branches tied, ready for delivery, Trace knew it far surpassed the spindly reject back in the truck.

"Let's take a peek!" Bending down, Monique straddled the tree, making her sweet round butt impossible to miss. *How was he supposed to control himself around her?*

Instead of reaching out and cupping one of those precious tight cheeks the way he wanted to, Trace rubbed his neck and enjoyed the show. "Need some help?

"Nah, I got this." She pulled a pocket knife from her jeans and sliced through the plastic ties around the tree, like a pro. "Voila," she said, in her own world, probably not noticing he was still there. Clutching the tree's trunk, she raised it a few inches off the ground. She repositioned her grip and tried to lift it.

"Hold on, it's twice your size. You're going to get that up and it'll topple over you." Trace moved to the other side, squatting near Monique. He brushed over the soft skin on the top of her hand as he grasped the trunk. "Here, let me help." Monique didn't let go of the tree. The muscles in her small hand tightened. "Please, stand back." When she didn't budge, Trace came up with another tactic. "You won't be able to thoroughly inspect it for the Santino winery, unless I hold it for you."

"Fine." Stepping over the tree, she pivoted, knocking him out with a beaming smile. Her eyes danced with excitement, and an overwhelming urge to take her in his arms and kiss her wildly overcame him. As much as Trace thought he'd forgotten all about her after she refused to join him on the road years ago, apparently he hadn't. Monique took a few steps back and stood beside Adele.

Tasting the acrid needles in his mouth and feeling resin on his hands, Trace adjusted his grip on the sticky trunk. After securing a tight hold, he heaved the massive tree up to its full height. The branches covered a five-foot diameter.

Monique squealed. "It's perfect."

Adele giggled. "It's the biggest tree ever."

Not able to see their expressions from behind the tree, Trace shoved the prickles out of the way, made room for his head, and poked it in between two branches for a peek.

With almost identical expressions, Adele and Monique both raised their hands to their faces trying to cover the same spectacular grins. Except for her darker hair color, Adele was the spitting image of her beautiful mother.

After setting the tree down and retying the branches, Trace found Joe in the lot. Under Monique's close supervision, of course, he and Joe hauled the twelve-footer to the pickup and placed it on the ground. Trace let down the rusted tailgate.

"Where should we put this one, Joe?" He grasped

the castoff by the stem and yanked it out of the pickup.

"Wait." Monique nailed him with the sexy gleam in her eyes he never could resist. *Is she flirting with me?* "I just remembered something." Her cheeks grew pink, and she covered a giggle with her hands. *She is most definitely flirting with me.* His body hummed. "You're going to kill me for this." She laughed. He'd almost forgotten how magical she sounded.

While mulling over options to lure Monique and her laugh into a date, her exotic blue-grey eyes worked like a magnetic field pulling him in closer. Acting on instinct alone, Trace clasped his hands around her velvet fingers and pulled them off her pretty face. Holding her hands now, he couldn't let go. "What? What are you going to kill me for?" Whatever it was, he'd die a happy man.

Unfortunately, Monique shrugged out of his grip and pointed to the snubbed tree. "Um—you actually delivered the right tree. Sorry…" She clocked him with another giggle. "Um, I ordered *two* trees. That's the one for the ladies' room."

Chapter 3

Trace pulled into the Napa Pines and Wines parking lot and shoved the gear in park while grinning. After transporting Monique, Adele, and both trees back to Santino Winery, she thanked him profusely and threw him for a loop by asking him on a date *before* he could ask her. Although he would've enjoyed partaking in a little one-on-one action without Monique's little girl nearby, Joe needed him back at the lot. But Trace wouldn't get on the plane to New York without seeing Monique again. When he asked if he could call her tomorrow, she gave him a killer smile and said yes.

Trace shut off the ignition and slid out of the truck humming. A cool fresh breeze whispered above, reminding him of the pleasures of small town life. *Monique.* She made the invitation to the Santino Winery party that evening sound like an afterthought, and suggested he might enjoy seeing the tree he worked so hard to deliver decorated. But Trace convinced himself Monique was only trying to find an excuse to kiss him.

Trace scooted around a line of customers in the Napa Pines and Wines gift shop. He'd left his suitcase, and more importantly Lola, the guitar he wrote his first song on, behind the counter under the cash register. He felt naked without her. He reached around Joe and grabbed her and the carry-on.

"Hey, you're that guy!" A man holding an infant gestured to him with his chin. "Honey." He bumped a woman near him with his shoulder. "That's the singer we saw on the TV special, am I right?"

"Guilty as charged." Trace slung the guitar case strap over his shoulder and gripped the handle of his suitcase. "Thanks for watching." Trace didn't have an issue performing in front of thousands blinded by the lights on a stage, but always became a little uncomfortable with one-on-one praise. Hoping to avoid any further attention, he kept his head down and moved to a darkened corner on the other side of the room.

While waiting for Joe to finish with the customers, sights, smells and sounds from his youth flooded his senses with memories. Under the shop's thick pine scent, "Jingle Bell Rock" played over a crusty boom box. Outside the door, a gaggle of new smiling arrivals entered the lot in search of the perfect tree.

The old register dinged, and the money drawer opened with a clang. Joe counted out some bills and gave them to the last beaming customer in line.

"Thank you, Joe. We'll see you next year."

After waving them off, Joe glanced over. “Ready for a chat?” He eyed the suitcase. “You calling it a day?”

“Yep. I’ll be right back. Need to put these away. I don't want to leave Lola all by herself.” He gripped the case’s strap. “Any word from Barb?” Trace asked on his way to the door.

“No, not a peep.” Joe wiped the counter with a rag. “Where you staying tonight?”

Taken off guard, Trace stopped. What an unexpected question for Joe to ask. Wasn’t he welcome to sleep in the bungalow in back, the same place he’d stayed for years? “I thought I’d crash in the cottage if it’s okay with you.”

Joe tossed the rag on the counter. Sighing, he came around to him. “Of course, it would be perfectly fine for you stay there, if—we need to talk.” Joe put a hand on Trace’s shoulder and led him out back. A customer waved, wrangling Joe's attention. “Can you give me five?” Joe asked, but kept walking. “I’ll be right back, promise.”

Joe didn’t take the usual footpath that wound behind the tree lot to the private area where the cottage stood. Instead he ushered him twenty feet behind the gift shop. Dangling white lights from the tree lot illuminated the area.

“What’s going on, Joe?”

"Welp, the thing is"—he kicked the ground—"the cottage, well, it isn't here anymore, Trace."

"What the hell are you talking about?" Trace set his carry-on on the ground and waited for Joe to explain.

"I'm real sorry." Joe scratched his head. "I guess I should've mentioned the fire." His lips were a straight line and thick crevices wedged into his forehead. "The bungalow burned to the ground with everything in it. That's what I wanted to talk to you about tonight."

The sucker punch came before Trace could brace himself. Joe could've delivered a kick in the teeth and the result would've felt the same. Without knowing why, Trace clutched his stomach and dropped his head.

Knotted pine counters, the old white fridge with the cracked handle, his grandmother's Christmas ornaments, and discolored photographs in his uncle's album flashed before his eyes. Those were some of the items he came to retrieve, others he would've said good-bye to before he sold the place. Trace jotted reminders to himself that morning during his flight from La Guardia to Oakland so he wouldn't forget.

"The fire happened last year, right after you left your uncle's funeral. Things were pretty hectic."

"How?" A vein in Trace's neck twitched.

"Vandals? That's what the inspector said, anyway. They never made an arrest." Joe wiped his forehead with his arm. "I don't know, maybe a copycat arsonist? You know about the Valley fire right before—"

"Uncle Glenn died, yeah I remember. Smoke clogged the air the entire week of the service." Trace drew a deep breath and loudly exhaled. "Jesus."

"I should've told you." Joe patted his shoulder. "At least it didn't spread to any of the trees. We didn't lose any inventory, thank God." He pointed to a ramshackle RV a few yards away. "You're welcome to stay in the castle."

The rusted shell appeared ready to collapse. Used to crashing on tour buses, and ready for a hot shower, Trace snatched his suitcase.

"I've got the keys right here," Joe said, pulling a set from his pocket and moving to the door. "Let's get you settled."

Sighing, and giving the accommodations a second thought, Trace kept his distance. He watched Joe struggle getting the key into the slot and tug the handle. The door creaked when it opened.

Joe stepped inside and raised his voice. "The bed's not too lumpy. I sleep here sometimes when Barb gets mad. Haven't changed the sheets in about a year though." He guffawed. "So they're broken in. Come," Joe beckoned, "make yourself at home."

Trace narrowed his eyes and adjusted the strap on his shoulder. He kept his feet firmly planted. Although not picky about accommodations, the distinct musty smell of mildew pouring from within the cabin made his stomach turn. The thought of sleeping on Joe's crusty sheets wasn't appealing either.

"You can wash up in the lot's bathroom. Water's not hooked up in here and she doesn't have power, so change while it's still light." A few loud thumps came from within. "There's a flashlight in here, somewhere."

Gripping his carry-on's handle, guitar strap over his shoulder, Trace eyed the heap on wheels. Drawing his hand to his neck, he stroked his Adam's apple deliberating. "You know, Joe?" Tilting his head, Trace massaged the tension in his jaw. If everything went according to plan, he'd have a date with Monique tomorrow. "I appreciate the offer, but I think I need to find another place." Joe popped his head out the door and raised his eyebrows. "It's just that I'm here for a week," Trace explained. "And after a few days, as comfortable as the trailer probably is, I'll need a place with a shower."

"Welp, suit yourself." Joe stepped out the trailer and locked the door. "Don't know if you'll find a place to stay nearby, Trace. The valley's booked up with the lighted tractor parade in Calistoga next week."

"I'll find someplace in Napa."

"Doubt it. Even the Napa Palace is booked.

Delivered their tree yesterday. They mentioned the tractor parade one time in *Sunset Magazine* and folks from all over the country are pouring in to see it."

Walking through the scented pines and maneuvering around the rows of trees in the busy lot, Trace steeled himself for a hotel room hunt, determined to make the three hour round trip from San Francisco daily, if needed. He pulled out his phone to start making calls.

"Sir, we found one, could you help us?" The customer Joe deserted ten minutes ago interrupted. "Please? My daughter needs to go to bed early for school tomorrow."

"Hold on." Joe pulled a phone from his pocket and pivoted to Trace. "Hold on to *you.* Don't make any reservations yet." He gestured to the woman waiting. "One minute." He held his finger up to her and then put it on his phone and punched a number.

Rolling his eyes, Trace second-guessed his decision to pass on Monique's invitation to the Santino Winery party. Even though she'd be working, he could be sipping a tasty Santino Syrah and gawking at her right now.

"You're all set." Joe stashed the phone back into his pocket. "I just texted you the address."

"Don't get me wrong. I appreciate the effort, but what sort of accommodations are we talking about here?"

"Bed and breakfast." Joe shrugged. "And before you ask, yes, they have a shower."

Chapter 4

A few miles up the road from Napa Pines and Wines, Trace found the sign on the Silverado Trail that read "Nana's Garden Bed and Breakfast. Clean beds. Hot breakfast and dinner for your wine country pleasure."

After checking into the lavender room, the only available suite in the inn, Trace took one of the longest, hottest showers of his life and tried not to think about the fire. He changed clothes and did what he always did when he needed to unwind: he unpacked Lola. Finding a comfortable position on the bed, he practiced a few new riffs he'd been trying. Lola wasn't an acoustic guitar, so when he didn't plug her into an amp, Trace could play anywhere without making too much noise. He didn't hear any complaints from the innkeeper, so he practiced tunes until the light faded over the vineyards.

Chuck Berry's "Run Rudolf Run" seeped into his suite, interrupting his song's melody. A low murmur of laughter and shoes echoing against hardwood floors below distracted him. But the mouthwatering aroma of chicken and onions is what persuaded Trace to tuck Lola away and investigate.

Spying over the staircase railing, he couldn't see any action but heard it clearly. A child's familiar laugh rang and she sang, "Run, Rudolf, run."

Taking two stairs at a time, he hurried down the staircase. "Mr. Trace! What are you doing here?"

"Adele?" He wanted to ask her the same thing, but she wasn't in the mood for talking or standing still.

Dressed in all-in-one pajamas covering her toes, she broke into a smile that took up most of her pint-sized face. With her curls flying and little feet barely touching the floor, she shrieked and tore straight at him. Seeing where her flailing elbows were heading, Trace bent down to protect his lower body parts.

He wouldn't have believed how sharp her elbows were until one connected with the area right under his rib. "Ohh!" She grabbed his arm and hung on swinging, practically dislocating it from the socket. "You realize I need that arm when I play," he teased. "Hi, Adele."

"Hi, Mr. Trace." Stretching her neck back, examining his face, Adele focused her blue-grey eyes on him, looking astonishingly like her mother. Then she poked him in the stomach with a sharp pointed finger.

"Hey. That's no way to say hi." Trace scanned the room for Monique. He thought she'd still be at Santino Winery. He never dreamed he'd see her here. "Where's your mom?"

"How many cookies did you have, Addie?" The woman who checked him in earlier placed her hands on her hips. "Trace Montgomery is our guest, dear. Please leave him alone."

"It's okay." In fact, Adele's jubilation over seeing Trace beat any welcome a stadium packed with fans could've given him. "I had the pleasure of meeting Adele today. I'm a friend of Monique's." Trace extended his hand. "It's nice to meet you properly."

"I'm Loretta, Monique's grandmother," she said, shaking his hand.

"She's my nana." Adele squealed, throwing her hands up to her face and laughing.

"Yes, I'm your nana and nanas know when their great-grandbabies have had too much sugar. Wash up now. Dinner's ready."

***

So enthusiastic about sitting down for a real meal in a homey dining room instead of having a bite at a road stop, Trace lingered for three servings of Nana's famous chicken and potatoes. Adele, Loretta and a few of the other guests kept the conversation light. But

Trace cringed when Loretta mentioned Monique's situation and how she had lost her house because of Jarod.

Never in a million years would Trace have expected to find her living in two small rooms in the back of her grandmother's B and B. Now he understood why she got so worked up about the tree today and hoped her party went off without a hitch.

After pumpkin pie, Adele dragged him into the living room to read. Trace eyed the entry hall. According to Adele, Monique's keys would rattle against the front door any minute.

He poured two glasses of wine and tucked into the couch in front of the Christmas tree near the fireplace.

"Got it!" Adele scampered over from the bookshelf, waving a book. She climbed on the sofa and wedged next to him. "See?" She pointed to a white puppy with brown spots on the cover. "That's him."

This was a first. Instead of playing with Lola upstairs, something he did almost every night, Trace was about to cheat on her with a puppy named Poky.

"*The Poky Little Puppy's First Christmas.*" Smelling like a fruit salad and soap, Adele sounded out and pointed to each word on the cover. Then she flipped to the first page and began reading aloud.

This was another first. Trace had never helped read a bedtime story or any other book to a child. As an only child from a small family, the opportunity never presented itself. Instead of being uncomfortable, he hazarded a guess as to when he'd become a father. Trace furrowed his brows, listening to Adele. *If* he met someone immediately and *if* he knew she was *the one* after six months of dating, he'd be off to a good start. *Then*, if she wanted to start a family too, and *if* she got pregnant right away, he'd be thirty-five when he became a dad.

He sighed, sinking deeper into the couch, enjoying the homey chicken and onion aromas leftover from dinner. Adele's soft, melodious voice lulled him. In the dimly lit room, the sweet red, green and blue lights on the Christmas tree began to blur. His eyelids felt heavy.

"What's this word?" Adele pointed her dainty finger to letters on the page. "I know this is a Y. Is it why-a-wh-ned?"

Trace examined the page. He stretched his hands above his head. Then linking his thumbs together, he arched his back against the pillows and yawned. "The power of suggestion." He winked at Adele. "It's 'yawned'. The Y sounds like yah."

Trace continued helping her sound out words while she read the book to him over and over until she could barely keep her eyes open. He couldn't remember the last time he felt so cozy.

"What are you doing here?" The sound of metal keys hitting a dish and a recorded, "Ho, ho, ho, Merry Christmas,"chimed from the entry. He swiveled his head around. Monique dropped her purse on the hall table.

Jabbing her knee into his thigh, Adele scrambled off the couch and bolted to her. "Mommy!" She threw her arms around Monique's leg.

Gripping Adele's bottom with both hands, Monique picked her up and snuggled her close. With Adele's arms around her neck and legs straddling her, they covered each other with kisses.

Smooch, smooch, smooch sounds filled the room. Trace stifled a smile, and not wanting to intrude, looked away.

"He's helping me read, Mommy!" Adele skipped to the couch and grabbed the book.

"You don't have to help her, Nana's here."

He grinned at the flickering sparks in her eyes.

Monique put her hands on her hips. "You're a paying guest?"

"I—Joe made the reservations. I didn't know you lived here, and it's no problem reading with Adele." Trace picked up his glass and took a sip of wine.

"Time for bed, Adele. Get going and I'll meet you in your room and tuck you in."

Adele tossed her book on the couch and stood in

front of him. Full of energy again with Monique's arrival, he didn't know whether she would come in for a hug or sock him in the stomach.

"Night, Mr. Trace."

"Sweet dreams, Adele," he said unable to stifle a grin.

She took off loping down the hall. "See you in the morning."

"How many of those cookies did Adele have?" Monique approached the couch, shrugging out of her jacket.

She'd changed out of her jeans for the party and wore a little black dress that displayed every curve. And, oh . . . slay him now. Monique had high heels on. The way her hips swayed over smooth, tapered legs with strides so long, lean and sexy made him wonder why she'd ever think about wearing pants.

"No idea. I wasn't counting."

"Is that wine for me?" Monique pointed to the glass on the coffee table.

"I poured it just for you." He scooted over and patted the cushion beside him. "Join me."

"Give me a minute to tuck in Adele. I'll be right back."

Chapter 5

Monique dried her face on the towel and glanced at the bathroom clock. In seven hours she'd start all over again. Facing a quick work turnaround tomorrow morning, she needed to get ready for bed. If Trace didn't want to have a glass of wine with her bare, makeup-less face, it was his problem. After changing into the least attractive pajamas she owned, the ones with the faded blue snowmen with unnerving faces, she ambled to her closet. If she accidentally let her guard down, she'd need extra fortification against Trace's possible roaming hands. Monique pulled a thick, fuzzy bathrobe covered with Santa hats off the hanger and put it on. After tying the sash in a knot, she traipsed into the living room.

"Ahh…" she said, sinking into the couch and bumping his arm. "This is much better." She propped her jingle bell sock-covered feet on the coffee table and reclined into the cushions. "You have no idea."

"Wine?" Trace handed her a glass. "So I take it you're not mad about me staying here."

"No." She tipped the glass to her lips and savored her first sip of the night. A subtle taste of berries covered her tongue and the mellow liquid trickled down her throat. "Joe texted me. I'm happy we—Nana—could take you in. She only rents four of the rooms here."

Trace leaned against her shoulder with his arm. Luckily her bulky bathrobe diffused some of the tingling sensations coursing through her body. It was a good thing she'd changed into fuzzy armor. If she hadn't had the presence of mind to get out of that cocktail dress, she'd be naked under the tree in no time. Nana wouldn't appreciate having heart failure.

Monique took another sip and tried to pretend the living, breathing aphrodisiac known as Trace wasn't sitting next to her. The second she'd read Joe's text about Trace needing a place to stay, she'd intended to avoid him at all costs. What possessed her to have a glass of wine with him in front of the tree?

It was nothing like the glamorous, fairy-lit wine bottle spectacle she'd decorated for the Santinos. Nana's handmade beaded ornaments, the white string Christmas tree Adele made at preschool, and other homespun collectables hung amidst colorful lights, making the tree ooze with charm. Congratulating herself on another job well done, Monique glimpsed at Trace. Above his well-worn jeans, extremely *well-worn*, a black V-neck T-shirt covered his impressive chest. His biceps looked ready to latch on to.

He raised a brow over his flashing eyes. “Are you going to tell me how it went tonight?”

“Smooth as silk. Well, my part, at least. Thank God, because Michael’s father and all of his brothers came. Of course, there were the usual suspects who drank a bit too much. And we didn’t anticipate calling so many extra cabs and Ubers to get them home, but I think, overall, Michael was pleased. Fingers crossed, I’m moving up from tour guide to promotions assistant.”

“They’d be crazy not to promote you.”

She sighed, happy he’d thought enough to ask about her evening. “I’m pooped. I don’t think I’ve ever decorated a tree or turned a rabbit into a reindeer so fast. Record time.” Monique reached down and rubbed her big toe. “I don’t think I should’ve worn those new shoes tonight though.”

“Here, I’m an expert.” Trace surprised her by moving her feet to his lap.

Clutching her right foot, Trace rubbed the bottom and worked his fingers into her sore tendons. Basking in relief, Monique mumbled, “I don’t think you know what you’re getting into, because if you keep doing that, I won’t let you stop.”

“Better?” He rolled his knuckles over her arch.

“It feels like heaven.” She started to close her eyes. “Please don’t bring me back down to earth.”

"Never."

Mesmerized by the expert touch of his strong hands, Monique shifted her arm and rested her glass on the table. Then, she repositioned her back against the armrest, allowing Trace full access to her aching feet. As pretty as those heels were, they were brutal. All at once she realized what on earth she was doing and pulled her feet away from his hands. Just because they used to date didn't give him the right to give her toes an orgasm. "Much better. My feet are good now. Thank you."

"Nice try." Trace locked a grip on her feet and brought them back to his lap. "The customer is always right." He leveled a sly grin. "Hey, I paid for a room. You said so yourself." Before she could say a word or yank her feet back, he tightened his clasp around them. "No moving."

Trace's forehead creased with his serious expression. She laughed at the way he narrowed his eyes, committing to hold on to her poor toes for dear life.

She sighed, relaxing again. Trace had the ability to calm her as fast as he excited her, like no one else. Monique closed her eyes and leaned back letting him press his thumbs against the balls of her feet. "Well, as long as you insist, my toes would like multiple orgasms please." He chuckled. "You have no idea how good that feels. Adele is always giving me foot rubs, but her hands just don't have the strength."

"You've had a rough day." Seemingly dedicated to the task of giving her pleasure, he placed her right foot beside him on the couch and picked up her left. Applying pressure, Trace started at her heel, and pressed his thumbs over her sole and up to the ball of her foot. He cleared his throat. "It doesn't seem like the past six years have been a walk in the park either. Why did you pick Jarod over me?"

She opened her eyes. "But I didn't." Shocked he'd bring Jarod into this sweet moment, Monique drew her legs up. She straightened her back against the armrest. "Why would you ask such a thing?"

"I didn't mean to make you upset." Trace shrugged, picking up his glass. "It's something I've been thinking about."

The fatigue from her day switched to a *Mayday, Mayday* alarm waiting for his response. Her heart pounded in her chest while he swallowed a sip of wine and placed the goblet back on the coffee table.

"Why do I ask?" He gestured to the entry hall leading to their bedrooms and she knew he was referring to Adele. Trace ran a hand over the cover of *The Poky Little Puppy's First Christmas* book beside him. "Adele's four. It doesn't seem like you wasted much time finding someone new."

She gaped at him. “I did—I mean—I didn’t.” Pressing her thumb and index fingers against her forehead, she hoped to relieve the stress knotting in her head.

Trace pulled one of her trembling hands away from her face and held it. “Enough time has passed.”

The corners of his eyes drooped, and he blinked several times. Monique could usually read his thoughts from his facial expressions alone. They used to joke about how he could never become a poker player because of it. But this time, Monique didn’t have a clue.

“I won’t hate you, I promise. No matter what. Just tell me why. The *real* reason.” His grip around her hand tightened. “Why didn’t you come with me, Monique?”

“I don’t know what to say.” Not able to maintain eye contact any longer, she studied his hand and the way his fingers curved around hers. At some point in their lives, she knew they might meet again and have this conversation, but had dreaded the thought. It took every ounce of her energy to focus on the future. She hated dredging up the past, and wasn’t prepared to have this discussion now. After Monique made the decision to stay home, Trace never called, never texted, or emailed. They never spoke to each other again.

"Try."

Monique closed her eyes for an instant, trying to get a handle on the right words. Then she sat up straight and looked him in the eye. "We only dated for six months, Trace, not that they weren't great months, they were." Of course she'd thought of him over the years… "But the gears changed quickly with your career. With your new manager, and album, contracts, the charts, tour dates . . . You were moving so fast. I couldn't catch up." She rubbed the back of her neck. "You wanted me to just jump on a bus, travel around the country, and leave my family. I wasn't sure. And then, with all of your new fans going crazy over yo—"

"You didn't trust me."

"I knew all about what the music industry did to couples." She shook her head. "It felt like a bad idea. Someone is always getting their heart broken and the shattered pieces are plastered all over the internet. I didn't want it to happen to me."

Trace shook his head and leaned back against the cushions, staring at the fireplace. "What did I ever do to make you mistrust me?"

"Nothing." Monique drew a breath, facing her chicken-heartedness. Trace was the most trustworthy man she'd ever known. His career made her skittish, the unknown had made her fearful, and she'd bailed. "I couldn't bring myself to leave with you." She rubbed his arm. "I *have* wondered though, what might've happened with us… but it doesn't matter now. It took a year for me to start dating Jarod by the way, and maybe it wasn't long enough to get over you. I *thought* I met him at the right time. I wanted to settle down and he seemed stable."

"Jarod seemed stable?" Trace tipped his head back. "More stable than *me*?"

"I didn't know about his gambling addiction, okay? Completely clueless." She blew a strand of hair from her face. "Trust me. I'm paying for every mistake I made with Jarod, more than you know."

Silence hung in the air for an exasperatingly long moment. Then Trace sighed, adjusted his position on the sofa and rested his hand on the armrest behind her neck. The skin on skin contact at the nape of her neck sent tingles racing through her. Monique didn't move until he pulled her up and adjusted her so her head nestled in the crook of his arm. His smooth bicep smelled of winter oranges and cashmere. The rims around his pupils were a deep emerald green.

Bringing his hand to her face, he brushed her cheek, scorching her skin with his fingertips. "You didn't trust me, Monique. That's the real reason you didn't come with me."

She struggled for breath and her heart pounded in a tangle of surprise and the pent-up desire she'd stored for six years. Trace's fingertips traveled to her jawline. He tilted her face up, making it impossible to hide from his stare.

"What does it matter now?" Her words came out all air.

"It matters to me." Trace brushed his lips against hers and she shivered. "Do you think you could you ever trust me?"

She wished she could lie and tell him what he wanted to hear, but told him the truth. "I don't know."

"What did he do to you?" The searing sensation of Trace's lips coming down on hers, struck like a match. Kissing her, Trace reached around her back, bringing her closer, covering her chest with his.

Monique clung to his shoulders and tried to push away the thoughts racing through her brain. *Why did I let him go without me? How many more days will he stay? How will I feel when he's gone?* The heat emanating from his lips spread instantly, burning through her.

Lost in a haze of emotions, the Christmas tree lights whirled and her head spun. His lips were softer than she remembered and he tasted like wine. With Trace's thick muscles against her, she gave way to the delicious feeling of his weight claiming her underneath him and pressing her back deeper into the couch. His tongue found hers and a moan escaped him, shooting sparks down her spine. Trace kissed her harder, more urgently. Set on fire, Monique poured every answer to his questions into her kiss.

"Wow," he whispered against her lips.

Staring into his burning eyes, she caught a breath. "I've missed you too."

***

After an hour on the couch with Trace, Monique barely made it out of the living room with her snowman pajamas intact. With her top unbuttoned under her bathrobe, she climbed into bed, robe and all. She plopped her head on the mattress and stared straight up at the ceiling. Then she fluffed her pillow and rolled to the side, trying to find a comfortable position.

Finally, she threw off the covers and got up. Light from the full moon drifted through the edges of the shade. Monique slipped out of her robe and buttoned her top on the way to the window. Giving up on getting five hours of sleep, she opened the shade. And although the temperature had dropped into the forties, she opened the window, hungry for fresh air and clear thoughts.

She refused to feel guilty about kissing Trace. Regrets were against her religion. Monique had managed to put Jarod behind her, despite all the lying, conniving and thieving he'd put her through. He'd sold her a line of bull when she agreed to marry him, and she owned it. Without making excuses, she'd continue cleaning up the mess she created until it disappeared.

Having Adele changed her. When Monique admitted to Trace she wasn't sure she could trust him, she hadn't been lying. And although she loved kissing him, becoming any closer to Trace, knowing he would leave in a few days, would be too much of a risk. As Adele's mother, she didn't have the luxury of making any more mistakes.

Chapter 6

Monique strolled into the smell of bacon in the kitchen at seven thirty-seven. Her heels clacked over the vintage black and white tiles on the way to the coffee pot.

Dressed for school, wearing black leggings and a plaid blouse with frilly cuffs, Adele sat at the table polishing off pancakes with Nana and Trace.

"Good morning." Trace winked. Wearing navy blue, with hair still damp from the shower, he looked fresh, tousled and entirely edible.

Although she usually couldn't function without coffee, the wink put every cell of her body into high gear. She opted to ignore the sudden energy blast and pretend last night didn't happen. *No more kissing.* Monique lifted the coffee pot and poured into one of the cups waiting for guests on the counter. "Did breakfast go okay this morning, Nana? Light crowd in here . . . Oh, good morning, Trace."

"Magnolia and Geranium rooms aren't up yet." Nana checked the antique metal wall clock. "The Edwards left early and grabbed a couple of muffins on their way out."

"Well I don't blame them for wanting *your* pastries." Monique winked at Nana and then, deciding she needed a kiss, strolled to the table and planted one on her cheek. "Honey, get your jacket, we're running late." On her way to the refrigerator, Adele scurried into her bedroom.

"I can take Adele to school if it would help." Trace flashed his sparkling eyes over his plate.

Deciding how to respond, Monique opened the fridge door, and pulled out a lunchbox. She placed it on the counter near the muffins. "Thank you, Trace, but Adele and I have a routine we need to stick to." She sniffed the pastry, determined it was one of her favorites, pumpkin, and wrapped it in a paper towel. She nonchalantly glanced at him. Rubbing his luscious bottom lip with his index finger, Trace stared out the kitchen window.

"Come on, Adele," she yelled, shoving the treat into her purse. "I'm going to be late for work."

Trace rose from the table and pulled keys out of his pocket. "Monique, I have a rental car. It's no problem for me to drive Adele to school. Then you wouldn't have to rush to the winery."

"I know it might not seem like it to you,"—Adele dashed to the counter and Monique made sure her dainty hands grabbed the lunchbox— "but I have this under control."

She didn't mean to sound ungrateful, but couldn't allow him to start taking over responsibilities. It would only confuse and upset Adele when Trace left. Her father let her down enough.

"See?" She smiled, hoping he knew she wasn't angry with him. "We're all set. We don't need any help, but thank you, Trace. Now, go kiss Nana good-bye, Adele."

Holding her lunch, with her red jacket buttoned to the top, Adele hurried to the table and grasped her great-grandmother's neck with her hands. Nana pulled her onto her lap, allowing Adele to place a loud kiss on her cheek. "Mama, can I give Mr. Trace a kiss too, since you really like him? I saw you kissing him last night."

***

Trace scolded himself for bringing up the past with Monique. With limited time in St. Helena, he should be focusing on settling his uncle's estate. Yet he couldn't help asking the question he'd only guessed the answer to for years. He appreciated her honesty. He had a feeling Monique didn't trust that his feelings for her were real. He agreed his career fast-tracked quickly. He could barely keep up with the demands himself. And he understood why she'd been reluctant to leave with him. At the time, her mom and dad were still living in St. Helena. But, when Monique confessed she might not *ever* be able to trust him, it flat out shocked him. On the other hand, her sweet lips and sexy mouth gave him an entirely different story when they kissed. Trace ran a hand through his hair.

Mountains of paper, overflowing trash on the floor, and at least twenty dirty coffee cups added another level to his unrelenting distraction. Why Napa Pines and Wines employees referred to the filthy eight by eight broom closet Trace had commandeered as an office was anyone's guess. The meeting with Jim Hill, the accountant Michael Santino had recommended, hadn't gone well this morning.

Ella Fitzgerald's dulcet pipes crooned "Winter Wonderland" outside the open door, lifting his spirit. As the music filtered in from the gift shop, thoughts of Monique's mouth seeped back into his brain. Instead of concentrating on organizing the desk as he'd planned, Trace invented lyrics to Ella's song to distract himself from thinking about her. He dumped another stack of junk mail into the recycle bin. *Monique's eyes are a glistening... Her sexy lips I was kissing...* Trace gathered the handful of binders Jim Hill left behind and shoved them back into the cabinet. *Her body so tight... I want more tonight... Kissing a Monique wonderland...* He slammed the cabinet drawer shut and stared at the popcorn ceiling.

"Did you guys ever get any mistletoe?" At the sound of her voice, Trace kicked the cardboard file boxes out of the way and rushed to the door. He poked his head out.

Clad in a navy blue dressy coat, Monique stood in front of the register with her back to him. She must store that cute hat in the car because he definitely would've noticed the blue beanie with the fuzzy ball on top, if she'd worn it this morning.

"So you missed me." Trace entered the gift shop. She spun around and he appreciated the sparks of surprise dancing in her eyes. All day long, he'd imagined every nuance of her lips he could remember. And like an answer to a prayer, or a light switching on in a dark broom closet, there she was.

"I'm just making a quick run. We need mistletoe for the tasting room. The customers have been asking . . . I thought you were out making deliveries today?"

"Joe's covering today. I'm sure we have some around here."

"Ah—we don't." Bent over, with his arms resting on the register counter Joe's nephew, Kyle adjusted his glasses and stuck his nose back in his unwieldy textbook.

Trace frowned. "Whatever it takes, we'll get some for you." He studied an empty shelf. "Maybe it doesn't grow around here."

"Yes it does. It's a parasitic plant." Sighing, Kyle closed his book with a *thwack.* After straightening his tall, lanky body to full height, he put his index finger on the glasses above his nose and pushed them into place. "Phoradendron macrophyllum is the mistletoe species commonly used at Christmas. But all American mistletoe species are native to California."

Trace caught Monique's eye and they raised their brows at each other. "I wouldn't have guessed you were such a kissing expert, Kyle."

"You're welcome." Kyle opened his book again and bent over the counter. "Ag major, UC Davis."

Shifting to him, Monique adjusted the shoulder strap of her purse. "It's not a problem, Trace." She rested her hand on his arm, and his chest tightened. "I'll buy it somewhere else."

"No, don't leave." Trace couldn't let her wiggle those hips and rumba out the door. He hadn't spent nearly enough time getting lost in her eyes or lusting after her phenomenal curves when she wasn't looking. Her body drove him insane, but that didn't mean he didn't want to stare at it for days. And besides, he hadn't tasted her lips yet today. "Let's hunt in the trees back behind the lot. I'm sure we'll find a bush near the redwood grove."

Monique pulled out her phone and scrolled through several messages.

Trace caught Kyle staring him down, probably about to override his plan with a plant specific factoid. Trace mouthed "no" to him.

"Everything seems to be okay at the winery." Monique put her phone in her purse. "I think I have some time."

Trace sighed with relief. Recalling the sexy little sounds she'd made kissing last night gave Trace the nerve to guardedly slip his hand into hers.

Instead of pulling away, Monique intertwined her fingers around his and led him out the door.

They cut through the Christmas tree lot and took the path to the old redwood grove. With no customers in sight and the only employee on the premises buried in a book, Trace grinned at a revelation. He had Monique all to himself.

"So, how was your day so far?" She glanced up from the path at him.

"I'd rather talk about kissing you."

Her eyes blazed for an instant and then she tossed her head back to take in the sky. "Tell me. You were going to meet with an accountant and a realtor."

He hadn't intended to bog Monique down with any of the details. She yanked on his hand. "I'm interested.

I love this place."

"I met with Jim Hill this morning. He wasn't happy with Joe's accounting system." Trace rolled his eyes. "He collected all the loose receipts, check stubs and notes he could decipher, and said he'd get back to me."

Monique kicked a dirt clod off of the path with the side of her boot. "I hope the new owners don't fire Joe."

Trace glanced at her legs and wished her boots didn't go all the way up to the knee because they covered too much of her creamy skin.

"They won't let him go. I'm putting a clause in the contract forcing the buyer to retain Joe's services until he retires. My uncle used to handle the business end. It's not Joe's fault I asked him to take over everything until I settled the estate."

They reached the edge of the Christmas tree farm and Trace stopped to take in the view of hundreds of pointed tipped trees of various heights and hues of green. Majestic Mount Saint Helena and the purple-blue Mayacamas mountains towered in the distance.

"Joe planted all of these trees from seedlings. And see those?" Trace pointed to a silhouette of redwood trees against the crisp blue sky. "That grove of trees front a vineyard my uncle used to own. It's what gave him the idea of naming the place Napa Pines and

Wines."

Monique leaned against his shoulder.

Trace squeezed her hand and something made him bring it up to his face and kiss the top of it.

Her beautiful lips curved up in a sly closed-mouth grin. She teasingly batted her eyelashes and then brought her hand down. Tugging his arm, she urged him further down the path. "We're supposed to find mistletoe, remember? Get back to your day. I want to hear all about it."

As much as he didn't want to admit it, Trace felt relieved to have Monique there to talk to. "After the accountant left, I took the opportunity to tour the property. I found litter behind the trees, tripping hazards, and burned-out lights. Obviously, there's a lack of inventory in the gift shop."

They rounded a lone oak tree and Trace watched to see if she had any reaction to the barren lot he'd checked out after his talk with Joe. Monique gawked at the burnt wood remains of the cottage and cocked her head up at him. Her eyes were the shape of her Nana's dishes.

"This is another issue." Letting go of her hand, Trace walked over the mounds of debris and turned. Monique shook her head and gaped at him. Even though the fire happened over a year ago, the smell of fried wood filled his nostrils.

"This," he grabbed a handful of soot, "is where the family cottage used to be. And all my childhood memories are right here." He let the grey residue filter through his fingers to the ground.

"Oh my god, Trace." Monique trudged over the ashes hurrying to him. She wrapped an arm around his waist scanning the area. "I remember the bungalow. Your Aunt Ellie used to bring Nana and me out here sometimes and she always had—"

"Gingerbread in the oven." He stared at Monique, touched she remembered his aunt. There was no one else to share his memories with except Joe. Overcome with emotion and embarrassed by his sudden reaction, Trace swallowed a lump in his throat. The awful ache in his heart came back with the knowledge that all of his closest relatives were gone.

"Don't." Monique draped her other arm around him. She held on, hugging, and they walked away from the remains. "Don't look back, Trace. It will only hurt you. You've got to move forward and make new memories."

He agreed, but what kind of future did he have? The only occasion he looked forward to was the release of his next album.

They picked up the path again and Trace glanced back at the bungalow site.

"I certainly won't be moving forward with this

property. I feel sorry for whoever buys this place."

"They'll be lucky to have it and will get the business into shape in no time. Remember the hay rides your Uncle Glenn used to have? I bet they bring those back." To Monique, every problem was solvable.

The furry ball on top of her hat bobbed as they progressed side by side to the shade of the redwoods. Monique grabbed his hand and his heart flipped for the fiftieth time. Trace couldn't stop smiling.

"You could bring back hot chocolate nights," she said, "stock the gift shop with ornaments and wreaths. . . . and mistletoe. Adele can have her picture taken with Santa *here*, just like I did and carry on the tradition. We wouldn't have to go to the mall. And you could rebuild the bungalow. You own the lot, the trees . . . everything that's important you already have."

Trace stopped and Monique took another step. He dragged her back with his hand. "Did you hear what you just said? *I* could bring back hot chocolate nights? *I* could rebuild the bungalow? *I* have everything I need?"

She shrugged, scanning the area, evidently anxious to change the subject. "Is there any mistletoe around here? I have to get back to work."

Trace wasn't about to tell her he didn't know what mistletoe looked like, not after she accidentally revealed she could imagine him living in St. Helena running the farm. The woman did crazy things to his psyche. He felt like singing.

“I think I found some.” He brought her to a plant that if you squinted, might resemble mistletoe in the dark. “See?” He bent over and snapped off a few sprigs.

“You have no idea what mistletoe is, do you?” Monique put her hand on her hips.

“Well, your customers probably won’t either after a few wine tastings.”

Laughing, she snatched the twigs from his hand and held them up to inspect. “I can’t take this weed and hang it over a doorway.”

“You’re right,” Trace said, inching closer. “We should test it out ourselves just to be sure. Be warned though, I'm positive what you have in your hand is the real deal.” Trace moved another step. “And although I’m not an expert, this lot has been in my family for years.” Excited by the way her eyes flashed, Trace could barely keep a straight face. He raised a brow and pressed. “My ancestors have passed the secrets of mistletoe down to me. It makes people do crazy things at Christmastime.” Monique backed up against a tree.

“Hmm. No place to run.” He smiled. “You hold the power of my lips in your hands.” Putting her hands behind her back, she locked her exquisite eyes on him and grinned. His heart somersaulted.

"Did you sleep at all?" Trace asked, hoping their kisses last night meant as much to her as they did to him. "Because I didn't. I tossed and turned all night thinking about the way you taste. And then I got to wake up and see you first thing this morning."

Without breaking the stare, Monique tilted her head up. Trace couldn't be sure, but from the way she was angling her body, she appeared to be daring him to kiss her.

"Of course I thought about you."

"And now here you are with some silly excuse about mistletoe when what you really want is to kiss me again." He took the sprigs out of her hand and held them over Monique's head. Her pretty eyes so full of mischief and heat made her lips impossible to resist. "See, it's working."

"Weren't you supposed to be making deliveries today?" Her mouth was so close to his face her breath whispered against his chin.

"But I am." Her skin smelled like warm vanilla and fresh, cool grass. He let his nose lead his lips to her cheek and he kissed it. "That's one delivery." Her cheek rose in a smile under his lips. He moved to the other side of her face and kissed her there. "There's two."

Monique reached up and cradled his face. His breath hitched. Pressing her soft curves against his chest, she tilted her head up and kissed him on the mouth. She nibbled his bottom lip, and he thought he'd explode.

"There's three," she whispered against his lips.

Trace let go of the mistletoe and wrapped his arms around her. Tired of holding back, Trace kissed her with the passion he rediscovered last night, wishing he'd done it the second he had seen her in the gift shop. Monique's sensual kisses fanned the flame. There was nothing on this planet better than kissing her. Trace should've flown in from New York for this kiss alone.

Matching fire with fire, she ran her hands up and down his back. He tipped her into his arms, in a deeper kiss. Monique slipped her tongue into his mouth and slid it against his. The move sent Trace's body racing from sixty to two hundred in less than a second. Wanting to feel her skin against his, he had to fight not to pull every piece of clothing off of her.

The fact he already loved her body and was very well acquainted with every delectable nook and curve made him shudder. Memories of how she felt when she trembled, the moaning sounds Monique made when she came, and the incredible ways they blew each other's mind in bed flooded his brain.

They kissed like they were starving for each other. Pressing her hands against his cheeks, she tugged him closer. Trace dreamed of kissing her a hundred times after last night. He couldn't stop himself from covering her cheeks with kisses and trailing down the delightful soft curve of her neck.

"I want you, Trace."

Her words sent his wits spiraling out of control, and Trace reached for the buttons of her coat. Maybe they could find a soft bed of needles and a little privacy.

Putting a hand on his, Monique shook her head. "I can't stay. I have to get back to work and pick up Adele. Missy, one of her friends from preschool, invited her to a birthday party today."

He swallowed a breath and put his arms around Monique's waist. Dropping his head to her shoulder, he nuzzled behind her silky hair. "Can I come to your room later?"

"No," she whispered. Her soft lips brushed against his cheek. "Nana's across the hall and Adele is next door. If anyone is visiting any room, it will be me."

Surprised and entirely enthralled by what she'd just suggested, Trace lifted his head from Monique's shoulder and mouthed, "Thank you God," to the fake mistletoe bush.

Chapter 7

Hot water from the tub's faucet warmed her toes again. Monique took a deep breath and submerged deeper into the vanilla bubbles. Lauren, the birthday girl's mom, served hotdogs and hamburgers to the kids at Missy's party, so Adele had come home with a full tummy and thoroughly exhausted. She fell fast asleep the moment Monique tucked her under the covers. With mommy duties on hold, Monique concentrated on Trace, not believing what she was about to do.

Trace had been right. After originally panicking over him being back in St. Helena and then having a subsequent conniption over making out with him in front of the Christmas tree, Monique now relived his kisses every waking hour. Although she'd needed mistletoe for the winery, she had gone to Napa Pines and Wines hoping to see him.

She opened the bathtub drain and, with the water gurgling, shaved her legs again.

Satisfied her skin was as smooth as it would ever be, she stepped out of the tub. Her knees shook. She hadn't dated or slept with anyone since Jarod and had never considered a one-night stand before. And, ex-boyfriend or not, that's exactly what Trace would be. With him leaving in days, anything that occurred tonight would have to be without strings.

She pulled a towel off the hook and reminded herself she didn't have to fall in love with Trace again to sleep with him. Men managed to keep their hearts in check all the time. And so could she. After buffing her skin with a towel, she rifled through the bathroom closet and found the most expensive lotion she owned tucked in the back of the shelf. She slathered the cream over her body and the scent of white tea filled the steamy room.

Admonishing herself for the idea of hiding under her comforter, she gave herself a pep talk. When would she have the chance to be with anyone who used to be in love with her? Who better to satiate her loneliness and need for company than Trace?

Although her brain had prevented her from leaving her family and going on tour with him, her body would've jumped on board in a heartbeat. Although Monique couldn't trust anyone in a long distance relationship after what Jarod did, she could let go of her anxiety for one night with Trace. Couldn't she?

She slipped into a light blue teddy she'd bought on sale last year and had never worn. The silk fabric brushing against her skin felt decadent compared to the warm flannel she usually wore. Monique had saved the ensemble for a special occasion that never happened. It was the only sexy piece of lingerie she owned that looked halfway decent on her. After having Adele, her breasts and stomach never bounced all the way back.

Monique strolled to her closet and squinted, perusing her options. The teddy came with a matching cover-up. But she didn't bother rummaging for it and decided to play it safe in case Nana or any guests were still awake and milling around. She pulled her trusty Santa bathrobe off the hanger and put it on. This time she didn't tie the sash in a knot.

Giddy swells of exhilaration and nerves coursed through her veins. Lightheaded even though she hadn't had anything to drink, she vetoed a second thought of chickening out and left the room.

Slinking quietly like the sex ninja she'd become, Monique tiptoed through the darkened hall into the living room. The crotch of her teddy was already damp between her legs from just the thought of making love to Trace again. Stifling a thoroughly inappropriate laugh, one that roared to the surface at precisely the wrong time when she got nervous, she checked the hutch for something to take the edge off. The lights from the Christmas tree illuminated the room enough for her to grab two glasses and a bottle of Michael Santino's killer cabernet.

Her footsteps creaked up the stairs. Monique peeked down the hall, praying none of the guests would see her standing in front of the lavender room. She inhaled a deep breath, felt it shudder through her lungs, and knocked. When she exhaled, Trace opened the door.

His devilish little smile made his lips curve up mostly on just one side. "I didn't think you'd come." He ushered her into the room, closed the door and took the wine and glasses from her. Placating her nerves, she leaned against the door while he put the bottle and stemware on top of a dresser.

"I didn't think I'd be here either." Monique chuckled. Before she could say, "Have you been waiting long?" Trace reached around her waist enveloping her in his muscled embrace and deliriously sensual cedar wood scent. She hadn't been held by anyone over four feet tall in years. This gorgeous, talented man wanted her and she'd forgotten what it felt like. In another instant, Trace ran his hand up her spine and cupped the nape of her neck, tipping her back for a deep kiss, making her gasp against his mouth. She knew it way back then, and he confirmed it now—God put Trace's lips on Planet Earth to kiss her. End of story.

With her head nestled in the crook of his arm, and his hand holding the small of her back, she sucked on his delectable lower lip, relishing his clean taste. Long-dormant butterflies buried inside of her woke up. A deep moan escaped his lips electrifying her. Trace slipped his tongue into her mouth and stroked against hers. A jolt shot through her and they picked up where they left off at the Christmas tree farm. There was no awkward fumbling or tentative first time lover queries about liking this or that. Their bodies were still in love.

The six years they had spent apart morphed into a two-minute span, or no time at all. Monique pulled him closer and kissed him harder. With his fingers on her jaw, Trace ran his tongue under her lower lip and worked his way to her upper, giving them equal time. She drew a breath and broke away from the kiss. "I'm—a little—out of practice." Her knees buckled and he tightened his grip around her. "My legs shook so much, I barely made it up the stairs."

"Monique, you never have to be nervous with me," he whispered against her lips. Then he kissed her on the cheek and gave her open-mouth kisses all the way down her neck. She arched her back, not believing the wonderfully thrilling sensations of her body coming alive again.

Moving her bathrobe off her shoulder, he sucked and nibbled on the warm skin that ached for his caress. His smooth cheek rubbed against hers as his kisses moved up her neck and around her ear. She thought she'd collapse. Trace tightened his hold around her. She clung to him as he led her backward to the bed until the mattress brushed the back of her legs.

"Do you mind if I unwrap my Christmas gift early?" His voice contained a smile

Monique didn't have the words to answer. She nodded yes and would answer the same to anything he wanted. Despite what she said to him last night, she knew in her heart she trusted Trace and always had. She wouldn't be with him right now if she didn't.

"You are my Christmas, Monique. The only gift I've ever wanted," he said untying the sash of her bathrobe. Before she could respond, another shudder tore through her. He eased the robe off her shoulders and it fell to the floor. Trace stepped back. His eyes were dark and took her in as if she were a frosted glass of water on a sweltering day.

Monique sucked in her belly and reached for the nightstand. "Let's turn out the light."

He clasped his hands around her waist over the light fabric, creating a jittery mass of electricity. "Don't even think about it."

"But, I don't look the same. I've had a bab—"

Trace put his lips to her mouth. "No," he whispered before kissing her. Covering her body with his, his heart beat fast against her as he leaned her back on the mattress. Between breaths and kisses he said,

"You're just as beautiful, even more…" And silly or not, she couldn't help but feel beautiful.

He kissed under her lingerie strap and meticulously pulled it down. Trace covered the bare area with his lips and traveled south to her breasts. She arched her hips against the hard bulge in his jeans, holding her breath in anticipation. Trace cupped her breast and made her delirious by circling her nipple with his tongue before taking it into his mouth and sucking.

"Trace." A whimpering ball of frenzied nerves, she sank further back on the bed.

He came back to her lips. Giving both nipples equal time, he rolled each one between his thumb and index finger and kissed her again. Heat shot through her. The agonizing quiet ember smoldering under the surface for six years was about to blow. She gripped his shoulders and moved impatiently against his groin.

Without breaking their delicious tongue dance, Trace made a path with his fingers from her breasts, over her belly to the crotch of her panties. He reached into the side and slid a finger into her, and then another. When he used his thumb, rubbing mind-blowing circles against her sweet spot, she clenched. *Wait.*

"I want to come together like we used to," she whispered, hoping he heard her. With her nervousness gone, nothing mattered except feeling him inside of her.

Trace took off of his clothes before she had enough time to ogle him thoroughly. In a blur, she recognized his same beautiful chest, same tight abs, and the same thin line of hair leading down to his magnificent—condom. She hadn't seen him put it on, but felt relieved she didn't have to ask. Her body tightened with anticipation when he came back and blanketed her with his thick muscled chest. Before she could wriggle out of the remainder of her teddy, he pushed the flimsy fabric at her crotch to the side. Trace slid against her swollen flesh, once, twice; she was panting so much with need, she didn't know how many times he rubbed against her. With her head in the stratosphere, Monique closed her eyes, wanting to savor every phenomenal sensation.

"So beautiful," Trace whispered, moving her thighs apart with his. He gripped her hips and glided inside of her.

"Trace," she called out, becoming unglued, amazed by the feeling. "We're still perfect."

"You feel unbelievable." He moved back and thrust inside her again.

She clamped her legs around him. Holding on tight, she kissed his shoulder. He sucked the curve of her neck, moving in rhythm. Tightening, she pulled him deeper inside her. Over and over he filled her until her eyes rolled into the back of her head and every spark she had and even those she wasn't aware of blasted through her body.

"Monique." He moaned, relaxing his body on top of her. "Oh my God, Monique," he said into the pillow next to her ear.

Feeling like an unset bowl of Jell-O, Monique reached around the back of his head and played with the hair at the nape of his neck. She laughed into Trace's cheek. "We are so good together."

He lifted his head from the pillow and braced himself on his elbows. "We always were." Not wanting to miss a second of bliss, she kept her eyes open and watched him lean down and kiss her.

Trace planted a kiss on her nose and dug both of his hands under her. In one swoop, he rolled over, moving her on top of him. Grinning, she climbed off and snuggled next to him on the pillow. "Look what we've done." She bent down inspecting the mangled blue material wrapped around her legs and tugged at the fabric.

"Such a shame." Trace brushed over her hand and wound part of the elastic around a finger until it snapped. "But it had no business covering your body like that." After repositioning her head on his chest, Trace smoothed the hair off her forehead. "I don't think you know how much I've missed you." He kissed her hair and whispered, "I can't believe I'm leaving in two days."

Monique closed her eyes, trying to block out his words and her feelings.

***

Hazy light streamed through the pattern of lavender sprays on the curtain fluttering in the breeze. Something she remembered she loved poked her backside. Would she be able to walk today? Trace's warm, muscled arm prevented her from moving. Supremely relaxed, she snuggled into the pillow, trapped in his arms. *What a way to go.* She closed her eyes and then opened them. "Oh my god, it's a school day."

Monique scooted out from under his arm and tumbled out of bed, darting to her robe on the floor.

"I have to get downstairs," she said, slipping it on. "Adele will be looking for me." She frantically tied the sash.

Trace propped himself up on his elbow, appearing every inch like the sex god he was. His rippling bare chest, tousled bed hair, and green eyes were more tempting than coffee after a hang-over. He rolled over to the bedside alarm clock and grabbed it. Fortunately for Monique, the sheets went with him, uncovering his luscious butt. On his stomach, thighs splayed, Monique wished she could forget mommy duties for just ten more minutes.

"It's only six-thirty." Trace set the clock down on the nightstand. He rolled over and put his hands behind his head on the pillow. She couldn't peel her eyes away from the treat protruding from his groin. He caught her staring and grinned. "Come back, Monique. *Monique, Monique, with eyes so sweet and skin I love —*"

"Oh no. Not lyrics." She giggled, remembering the way he used to sing to her. "If you start making songs up about me, I'll never leave."

"Please." He patted the mattress.

She sighed because she couldn't resist and settled on the bed by his thigh. "Santa's got to go." Trace tugged at her robe and raised a brow.

"I should be downstairs already." Monique's hard nipples protested. Now that Trace had her engine running smoothly again, boy, did she want to go for another spin. "Nana's probably up making breakfast and Adele needs me to help her get ready for school."

"She has to go to preschool today?" Trace frowned. "It's the day before Christmas Eve. Why don't you let me take her today?" He reached under the robe and caressed her thigh. His hand inched higher. "We'll go Christmas shopping or something."

Barely able to focus because his fingers set off sparks through her veins, she moved his hand out from under her robe. "I wish I didn't have to take her, and thank you for your offer, but Adele should stay on her schedule." Monique couldn't bring herself to tell Trace she wanted to spare Adele the pain of missing him. She couldn't risk causing her any heartache. "We have a private party at the winery, so it's going to be busy. I'll only worry about her, and I don't want to put you out. I'm sure there are loose ends at the lot you need to wrap up."

"Nothing more important than you." His eyes flashed a sweet heat, and her heart tore at the seam. He brought her hand to his lips and kissed it.

"Adele will be all right at school. Nana made cupcakes. They're having a party."

Traced sighed. "Jim Hill is giving me the financial rundown today, and I have a few errands to do. So, I'll see you at dinner then?"

Monique let the invitation hang, not sure how to proceed. Her synchronized plan of keeping her emotions in check jettisoned out the window last night the second he kissed the straps of her teddy away from her shoulders. Trace would leave tomorrow, so a romantic one-on-one dinner with him was out of the question. It would only make saying good-bye worse, but she could manage dinner with Nana and Adele. She'd be home anyway. "Yes, I'll see you here tonight. We can say good-bye after dinner."

Chapter 8

Jim Hill's financial recommendations didn't surprise Trace. He left Napa Pines and Wines soon after the meeting. Deciding not to wait until dinner to see Monique, Trace drove to Santino Winery hoping to surprise her and take her to lunch. When he saw how busy the parking lot was and that every surrounding space on the adjacent roads was taken, he changed his mind.

Maybe she hadn't been exaggerating when she told him she had a busy day planned. Trace didn't want to intrude on Monique at work, but he needed time alone with her before he left. He had a nagging feeling she pushed him away at breakfast and it made him nervous.

Didn't Monique feel the undeniable connection between them last night? Wasn't it more than a random reunion between two lovers for her? Monique's touch, her velvet skin, taste, smile, mouth, curves, laugh, their shared memories, everything about her haunted him today more than the first time he met her.

Although Trace had protected his heart by not calling and hadn't begged her to join him on tour after she'd refused, he'd never forgotten her. She'd always be the one that got away. The only woman he couldn't completely have. And now, after being in St. Helena for only a week, Monique was the only person left on the planet he loved.

He spent the afternoon alone in Napa in a mass of hand-holding cheerful couples and families at the mall. Trace returned to St. Helena with Monique and Adele's Christmas gifts wrapped and hidden in the trunk of his rental car.

He ran a hand through his hair and strolled through the produce aisle of St. Helena Market in search of cards. Scooting around a display of fifty-percent-off poinsettias, Trace rounded a corner. While Burl Ives serenaded him from overhead with "Have a Holly Jolly Christmas," he found the display of greeting cards.

Thumbing through the good-bye section, he pulled a card and read: *Don't let the door hit ya, where the good lord split ya.* Trace returned it to its slot and chose another. Blank on the inside, it featured a puppy crying in the rain on the front. The dog looked too damn sad. The hollow feeling in his chest grew.

Why did he always have to say good-bye? The whole damn St. Helena trip was one pathetic farewell. Adios to the Christmas tree lot. Ciao to the bungalow and the memories. Adieu to his uncle, and now, so long Monique, bye-bye Adele. He spun the display around and studied the holiday greetings. He found one for Adele and picked out two different cards for Monique. He'd decide which one to give her later. Monique would be home soon and he didn't want to waste what little he had left.

***

Trace entered the dining room at seven. Loretta, Monique and Adele were already seated at the table. He slid into a chair across from Monique without taking his eyes off her. She wore her hair down and had a white sweater on that hugged her curves. He swallowed a lump in his throat and tried not to stare. After tasting her last night, he couldn't help dreaming about a second helping.

"I helped Mommy set the table." Adele pointed to white roses and green foliage tucked between the candles.

"It's very pretty, Adele."

"Mommy said we could light the candles because it's your last night. Are you leaving?" "I'm afraid so." Trace didn't think he'd ever get over the way Adele cut to the chase.

"I'm going back to New York tomorrow." Ignoring the heavy feeling invading his chest, he kept his tone light. "Have you heard the news?"

They gave him blank stares. "Jessica had a baby girl at five fifty-seven. Joe's a grandfather."

"Everyone okay?" Monique asked.

"They're doing great. They've named her Bell."

Adele's eyes got big. "Like Christmas bells?"

"I'll bet it is."

Loretta passed him a plate of lasagna. "Eat as much as you want. All the guests checked out, so we've got the place all to ourselves."

"What's the word from the accountant?" Monique picked at her plate. "How'd it go?"

Trace wiped his mouth with a napkin. "The farm doesn't earn enough to pay the taxes on the property. The value is in the land. But I'm not surprised. Let's not talk about it now, it's almost Christmas. Adele, what do you want from Santa?"

"I want Mommy to smile everyday like she is now." She giggled. "And Daddy to visit." She picked up her fork. "If you stay, you can meet him."

Trace threw a glance at Monique hoping she'd help him. "That would be nice." He didn't know what else to say. Jarod wouldn't make it for Christmas. According to Monique, he'd missed it every year of Adele's life.

"You're welcome to stay with us for Christmas, Trace." Loretta picked up her wine glass and held it to her lips. "Just because the other guests have left doesn't mean you have to go. I don't want you to think we're kicking you out." She sipped from her glass.

He fiddled with his napkin, feeling Monique's eyes burn a hole in his forehead. "Thank you. I appreciate the offer, but Dirty Harry needs me."

"What?" Adele asked, giggling.

Monique laughed. "You still have that stinky cat?"

"Dirty Harry is nine now and not half as smelly as he used to be. Turns out I was feeding him the wrong food. I may change his name to plain old Harry."

"So it's just plain old Harry and you?" Loretta asked.

Trace chuckled. "We make a good team. Harry's into the 49ers. He's a little quiet, but I wouldn't trade him."

While they ate dinner Trace chimed in when he could but mostly listened to their plans for the next day. They'd finish baking cookies, deliver them to friends and go to Christmas Eve mass.

Trace tried to sell himself on the beauty of New York and Rockefeller Square at Christmastime, but felt a tug and longed for the days his parents were alive. He managed to keep a smile on his face so they wouldn't notice how hard it was for him to hear about all the homey traditions he'd never take part in again.

When Loretta asked Adele to help her clear the table, he waited until they were out of earshot. "Do you want to join me someplace quiet? The living room?" He leaned across the table to Monique. "My room, perhaps?"

"I've been thinking about what to say all day." She smiled and Trace got his hopes up. "I don't think I want to go through another good-bye with you." She reached over the white tablecloth between the flowers and candles.

Trace held her hand. "I didn't mean for this to end this way, Monique. We've barely started. I want to keep seeing you. We don't have to say good-bye."

"I'm sorry." She chewed on her luscious bottom lip. "But I'm not a long distance kind of woman. I know myself well enough to know I couldn't handle it." Her eyes glistened in the candlelight.

The thought of Monique welling up, or, God forbid, crying sent Trace out of his chair and around the table in an instant. He crouched by her knees. "I don't want you to be upset," he explained, rubbing her leg. "Please Monique, what can I do?"

She cradled his face. Trace stared into her eyes, but didn't feel a connection. Her spark for him had flickered out. In a matter of a day, he'd lost Monique again.

"Maybe you should pack. Let's not make this any more difficult. We'll say goodnight now and tell each other good-bye tomorrow."

***

After practicing blues chords on Lola because he just couldn't help himself from wallowing, Trace spent the night flipping from one side to the other on his mattress. He mulled over every *what if* and *maybe* scenario he could imagine regarding Monique. Not wanting to face the reality of leaving, he waited until nine to get out of bed and dragged himself to the shower. While getting dressed, his brain continued its silent bombardment of options. One obnoxious voice yelled at him, demanding he stay in St. Helena, the other whispered *she's just going to dump you again.*

Maybe he didn't have to make a decision. Perhaps the airline would do it for him. Trace checked his departure time. It wasn't unheard of for flights to be cancelled on Christmas Eve, especially those heading to LaGuardia. His heart raced while he scrolled through the airline app in his phone. If it were cancelled, he'd be forced to lengthen the trip at least one more day. He groaned. Unfortunately, the plane was scheduled to leave on time, departing out of Oakland at one o'clock.

Shrugging, he grabbed Lola and his carry-on and packed them in the trunk of his rental. Stopping in the kitchen on the way back to the stairs, he looked for Monique. Seeing no reason to hang out since she wasn't there, he politely passed on the breakfast Loretta offered.

Back in the lavender room, Trace examined the space for anything he might've forgotten. He'd left nothing behind except Adele and Monique's gifts. After scooping them up and balancing the boxes in his arms, he trudged down the steps and into the living room. Monique and Adele were nowhere to be found.

Sighing, he knelt in front of the Christmas tree and scoped out the perfect location to deposit his packages. He wished he could be there to see Adele's eyes light up in surprise when she spotted his present. Trace tucked the gift under one of Loretta's bright gold beaded ornaments, next to a holly-covered package from Arizona.

"You didn't have to buy any presents." He swung around to Monique. She had her hair piled up in a bun and strands of honey colored hair tumbled around her cheeks. In jeans and a white T-shirt, she took his breath away.

"This one's for you." He held up her gift and

placed it in front of the pile. "Please open it at eight o'clock tomorrow morning. It will be eleven in New York. We'll think of each other at the exact same time on Christmas morning."

He straightened and held out his arms. "Monique, please. This is killing me." She shrugged and came to him, and nestled into his shoulder. "Why does it always have to end this way?" Trace let go of a shuddering breath and buried his head into the curve of her neck.

"I don't know. I could never figure it out," she said, wrapping her arms around his waist. Before he could tell her, before he could form the words, Monique surprised him and raised her voice. "Let me walk you out," she said patting him on the back. "Adele, Nana, Trace is leaving." She pulled away and he couldn't tell what was running through her brain. She didn't appear upset. "I don't want a big emotional good-bye, okay?"

This wasn't his plan. Trace thought they'd have a private moment and make arrangements to see each other again.

Adele barreled into the room with white powder covering the front of her sequined Christmas kitty shirt. Loretta trailed behind.

"If you can wait another ten minutes, you can take some cookies home with you," Loretta offered.

"Thanks, Nana." Monique grasped Adele's hand. "But Trace has to catch his flight. We don't want to keep him."

"It's been a pleasure, Trace." Loretta extended her hand, but he gave her a hug anyway.

"Thanks for everything."

Trace crouched in front of Adele. His eyes welled and he blinked back unexpected tears. "I'll tell Dirty Harry you said hi." He tapped her nose with his index finger. And just like he'd seen Loretta and Monique do during his stay, he wrapped his arms around her and straightened lifting her up with him. He brought her to his face and Adele's kiss on the cheek broke his heart with the sound alone. After kissing her, Trace quickly put her down, hoping to avoid a crying jag because it would only make this ordeal worse. What was he thinking? Nothing could be worse than this.

"Come on, we'll walk you to the car." Monique had either practiced her cool and even tone, or his departure was as insignificant as going to the mailbox. When she opened the door, "Ho, ho, ho, Merry Christmas," sounded from the umbrella stand. She left it open for him and strolled hand in hand with Adele to the rental.

Trace shifted to Loretta one more time and threw a reserved smile before following them. The little bell clanged against the door when he closed it.

"I don't have to rush," he explained, hurrying down the walkway to catch up. "I've got four hours before my flight. Did you ladies want to grab a coffee?" When he reached the car, he leaned down to Adele. "How 'bout a hot chocolate?"

"Thanks, Trace, but we've got a busy day of baking and delivering cookies. Don't we, Adele?"

Adele rubbed her tummy and nodded.

Not knowing what else to do, Trace punched the key fob and the car beeped. "I don't want to leave."

Monique's chin began to tremble and she blinked, tilting her head up to the clouds overhead. Why didn't she ask him to stay?

With his back against the car door, Trace folded his arms across his chest, waiting. He wasn't going to leave without a kiss.

Monique finally came back to him and he thought he'd never let go. She circled her hands around his neck and rested her cheek on his shoulder. Fresh rain and warm vanilla wafted up from her hair and he nuzzled against it. Not able to wait any longer, he inched back, searching for her lips.

When he tilted her face to his, Monique brought her fingers to his mouth. "Not in front of Adele. Not like that."

"Do you mind if I kiss your mommy?" When he saw how big and round Adele's eyes had become in response to his question, he decided against kissing Monique the way he wanted to. He gave her an unsatisfying closed mouth kiss instead, and pulled away before he couldn't stop himself from going in any deeper. He was already drowning.

Breaking away, Monique opened the car door. She held it for him, shuttling him inside like she couldn't wait for him to leave. After he climbed behind the wheel, she shut the door. The sound of the metal lock engaging had a finality to it that made his stomach drop.

Trace rolled down the window and only then saw her tears. His chest tightened, the lump in his throat became a fist and he fought for composure. "Don't forget, open my present at eight," he said to Monique before turning to Adele. "I left something under the tree for you. I hope you like it."

"I will!" She jumped up and down.

Without another option, Trace started the car and put it in drive. He tentatively drove down the street, waving out the window.

Adele yelled, "Don't forget to wish Dirty Harry Merry Christmas." He kept checking the mirror until they were gone.

Chapter 9

After delivering the last batch of Christmas cookies and going to mass, Monique, Nana and Adele sat in front of the tree in their pajamas. Monique had let the fire peter out earlier because Adele was afraid Santa would burn his boots when he came down the chimney later. Exhaustion set in right after Nana finished reading *The Night before Christmas.*

"I think Santa will like this one." Adele selected a green sugar cookie in the shape of a bell from the platter on the coffee table. Holding it, she skipped to the fireplace hearth and placed it on a plate next to a handful of carrots.

Eyeing the box Trace left for her, Monique put her elbows on her knees and nudged Nana. "Okay, Adele, pick out one present and then it's bedtime. You need to be fast asleep before Santa comes." She shook her head, smiling and aching at the same time. Adele had grown so much this year, she didn't want to ever lose these precious moments with her. A part of Monique wanted Adele to stay four years old forever.

Crouched beside the tree in her red onesie elf PJ's with pointy feet, she selected a large rectangle box with Christmas tree wrapping. "This one?"

Monique nodded. "Let's see the card." She put her hand out. "Bring it over and I'll help you read it."

Adele skedaddled to Monique and climbed onto the couch. Nuzzling into her side, she excitedly opened the envelope. Thumping her legs against sofa frame, she pulled the card from the slot, slowly revealing a picture of an orange cat dressed as Santa. Adele grinned and peeped inside.

While pointing to each individual word, Monique read them with her. "*Adele, Orange you glad, it's Christmas? Merry Christmas, Trace. PS: Lola wanted you to have this. I hope you like it. She needs a name.*" Monique tried not to regret her reserved farewell to Trace. She didn't have a choice. Any other method would've torn her apart. Maybe they'd see him again when he came back to handle the sale of Napa Pines and Wines.

Adele left the card on the sofa and shimmied back to the tree.

Monique fondled the card and reread it, brushing her fingers over Trace's handwriting. The crinkly sound of paper ripping made her turn. Adele broke into a fit of laughter, holding up a box with a picture of a pink guitar covered with daises. "My own guitar." She jumped up and down. "My own guitar."

Monique grabbed a Christmas tree cookie and bit

down. Sugary morsels melted in her mouth. She wiped a few crumbs off the front of her Santa hat bathrobe. She should've given Trace something for Christmas. Then she remembered the way he unwrapped her. *He called me his gift.*

"Let me help you with that, honey," Nana said, taking the box away from Adele and opening it for her with a scissors.

Adele held her breath, clapping while she waited. Her feet came off the floor and she shrieked when Nana handed her the gloriously pink instrument.

Adele immediately tucked it under her arm, strummed the strings and started dancing. "What should I name her?"

"You can dream about it when you sleep tonight. And let's not forget to thank Trace. Come, my little elf, let's bring it upstairs."

After tucking Adele in bed with Daisy the guitar beside her under the covers, Monique said goodnight to Nana in the hallway. She moseyed into the living room and finished preparing for Santa's big arrival. She wished she could've done more for Adele, and held out hope Jarod might drop by with something. A card would be nice. She tried not to think about Jarod's shoddy behavior and counted her blessings.

Adele had more love than a lot of children and plenty of gifts. Several festively dressed packages from

Nana and Monique's parents were under the tree. Of course, Trace had already made quite an impression. Monique made a path from the fireplace to the tree, using the few brightly wrapped goodies she'd bought for Adele over the months. Then she scattered cooled coals around the hearth, making it look like Santa's boots had traipsed over them delivering presents. After filling Adele's stocking with a chocolate Santa and candy, she plunked onto the sofa.

Monique eyed the present Trace left for her and gave in to temptation. She crept to it, picked it up and analyzed the shape. Bringing it up to her nose, she sniffed, but smelled only the ink from the Christmas tree covered wrapping paper. Holding it in both hands, she shook it. There was something, or *things* rattling and brushing against the inside of the box, but she didn't have a clue what it was. Monique felt for the seam in the cardboard under the wrapping. Cramming her nose into the crevice, she took another whiff. *Nada.* Scolding herself for acting like a crushing teenager, she put the box down and shoved it back under the tree. She'd keep her promise to Trace and wait to unveil the mysterious gift until tomorrow morning at eight.

Christmas Day

The mattress bounced from the weight of a small person who smelled of strawberries. The sleepyhead crawled on top of her and pried her eyelids open with two little fingers.

"Mommy." Adele's breath caressed her nose. "Mommy, wake up." Tiny hands massaged her back and pushed. The mattress wiggled again. "I wonder if he came."

Monique rolled over. The red Christmas elf pajamas made Adele's cheeks look extra rosy. Her curls dangled every which way.

Adele brought her hands to her face and laughed. "Hurry, Mommy!"

Thrilled that her daughter remembered the rule to not go downstairs without her, Monique threw off the covers. "Merry Christmas, sweetheart." She tore after Adele, caught her by the waist, picked her up and covered her with kisses. "You've been so good this year, let's see if he came."

Holding her elf tight, Monique reached the bottom of the stairs and let Adele scramble to the tree. Early morning light filtered into the room.

"Merry Christmas." Nana's eyes twinkled. "I've been up since seven."

Adele gave her a smooch on the way to the tree. "He came! He came! And look, he ate the cookie. And the reindeers chewed on the carrots!"

Monique eyed the platter of gingerbread cake and coffee, then deposited a kiss on Nana's cheek. "Merry Christmas." She sat on the couch and watched Adele open her presents: two Fabulista dolls with two sets of fashion packs from her grandparents in Arizona, a Harold Bear plush doll from Santa, a set of books from her and purple pansy covered plastic dinner plates, cups and saucers from Nana. Thankfully, Adele didn't seem to notice there wasn't anything under the tree from her father. While Adele decided which toy to play with first, Monique grabbed the carafe of coffee from the table and shuffled into the kitchen to refill the pot.

"Ho, ho, ho, Merry Christmas," rang from the umbrella stand. The bell clanged on the door. Holding the pot of coffee, Monique rushed down the hall and gasped. Bright-eyed and energized, like he'd been awake since dawn, Trace stood in the doorway wearing a navy blue sweater, jeans and a grin.

"W-What?"

Before she heard an answer he rushed over and kissed her. Instead of dropping the coffee pot she set it on an entry table and locked him in her arms.

"I don't understand what's happening." She squeezed him.

He beamed down at her. "I made it to the Napa Palace Hotel."

"Thank you for my guitar, Trace." The bells on her toes rang and her elf hoodie bounced as Adele jumped for him.

He scooped her up, planting a kiss on her cheek. "Merry Christmas." Flabbergasted, Monique stood gawking. "The hotel had room, it was practically empty. Never made it to the airport."

Monique circled her arms around his waist, and ushered him to the living room. "I don't understand."

Nana gathered a few play cups and saucers off the floor. "Merry Christmas, Trace. Happy to have you back." She winked. "Come on, Adele. Let's put your new dishes in the kitchen, we'll find a special place for them."

"Please sit down." Monique wasn't about to give him space. She stayed glued to his side and snuggled next to him the second their bottoms hit the couch. She had to stop herself from climbing on Trace's lap, straddling him and covering him with kisses. She waited until Adele and Nana left the room and asked, "What about Dirty Harry?"

"He's fine." He tucked an arm around her

shoulder and squeezed. "The neighbors will watch him for a few more days, weeks, or until I go back and get him."

Smiling so hard her cheeks ached, Monique tried to process the situation. She gaped at the tree, nodding with her mouth open. "So you're staying?"

"I don't have another tour planned, Monique. I have to put another album out first. There's nothing keeping me in New York, nothing that matters anyway." He moved his hand to the nape of her neck and tangled his fingers in her hair. "I thought I'd sit tight for a while. I have more *important* issues to focus on." He shifted to face her.

The flirty sparks of fire in his eyes held an answer. Hummingbirds launched in her stomach, waiting to hear what he said next.

"I've been thinking about us, about everything. I even did preliminary research on the effect of music on trees." He laughed. "Lola and I had some alone time at the hotel." He kissed her forehead. "Did you know some botanists believe trees grow faster when they listen to music?"

Delicious surges of excitement raced through her. "So, you're…?"

"And I thought about the last time we said good-bye." Trace shook his head, hesitating. "It was because I left on tour and you wanted to stay here. Instead of asking you to leave, Monique, maybe I shouldn't have gone. If I hadn't, I have no doubt we'd still be together. I'm not making the same mistake twice." He grasped her other hand. "So, yes, I'm staying. If that's what you're asking." He glanced at the box under the tree. "Now, open your gift."

Monique scooped up the big box and brought it back to the couch. She checked with him and he squinted his eyes at his watch chuckling.

"It's eight. I like your time zone much better."

She considered unwrapping the present neatly, then tore the gift wrap off and opened the box. Monique's heart did a pirouette and twirled. Hundreds of mistletoe sprigs tied with red ribbon filled the box to the rim. She couldn't stop smiling. "It's real?"

"I asked our friendly agriculture major, Kyle, to help me find it, so I can guarantee it's genuine mistletoe." He gave her a sexy lopsided grin. "Now, you'll never need an excuse to kiss me."

Her eyes filled with tears. Monique couldn't blink fast enough to hold them back. "Now, look what you did." Trace snatched a white envelope from the pile of discarded wrapping paper. "You didn't even read the card. Good thing." He shoved it in his pocket and pulled out another. "That one only said *Merry Christmas*, which is fine." He pulled her closer and covered Monique's cheeks with kisses.

She closed her eyes for an instant, wanting to take in every second of the magic. "Merry Christmas, my love," he whispered.

"Merry Christmas, *Love*?" Monique leaned and kissed him on the lips.

"This is your *real* card." Trace brought the envelope to his lips and kissed it. The corners of his lips curved up, making his eyes crinkle at the edges. "Remember when we walked to where the bungalow used to be and you said I need to think about the future when we were at the Christmas tree farm?"

She nodded.

"You told me I need to start making new memories. So here." His eyes threw a million sparks. "Open it."

Laughing, Monique beamed back at Trace. She pulled the card from the sleeve and smiled at the beautiful couple dancing under mistletoe on the cover. When she turned the flap, the music startled her.

She glanced up him and then read the message: *Trace loves Monique. I hope she loves me too.* And a little band inside the card played "What Are You Doing New Year's Eve?"

Just a Kiss

Barefoot, Sarah Dupont hurried to the kitchen, grabbed a handful of grapes and peeked through the glass doors at the rolling hills shimmering with grapevines. She still couldn't believe she lived here. Juliet St. John, Bella Villa's most recent resident, and Danica Vargas, Sarah's best friend, were huddled close together in deep conversation on the patio. Every afternoon from four to six o'clock in the summer, the women met for Chill Hour. Sarah found her favorite wine glass and rushed out to join them. When she reached the group, Danica and Juliet abruptly stopped talking.

"What?" Sarah asked. "Why did you get so quiet?"

Juliet raised a brow to Danica and gave Sarah an innocent smile. "Have a seat," she said patting the cushion on the chair next to her. "Go ahead, Danica, tell Sarah exactly what you just told me."

Sarah sighed, settling into a wicker chair. "Okay, here we go."

Danica poured the Rombauer Carneros Chardonnay into Sarah's glass, huffing while she waited for her to sip.

"I don't know what the big deal is," Danica said, tossing her hair and glaring at Juliet.

"Out with it," Sarah said.

"I have a fabulous idea for the Vine Café, that's all." Danica leaned close to Sarah. "You'll get loads of buzz on the internet for sure, maybe some free print, and who knows, Juliet will probably interview you on her morning show."

"And Danica gets a date with Michael Santino in the process." Juliet looked smug. "Don't leave that part out of the equation."

Danica's eyebrows shot up. "I didn't do it for a date and you know it."

"Of course you did, why else would you do it?" Juliet snipped.

Sarah waved her arms. "Hello! I'm right here."

"I knew it would help Sarah that's all," Danica said.

"Right." Juliet shook her head. "You were near Michael Santino and were only thinking of Sarah? Like that's even possible."

"What wasn't for a date?" Sarah asked.

"I didn't do anything. I would never do anything involving you or your business without asking first. I just had a little idea." Danica scanned Juliet, moving her chair even closer to Sarah's. Danica, the entertainment features reporter for the Napa Sun newspaper, made it her business to know all of the wine country's movers and shakers. "I saw Michael at the Santino Winery today and we started talking about Jamie. You know Michael's younger brother Jamie, right?"

"There are so many Santino brothers, Danica." Sarah peered into her glass. "He's the actor?"

"A very good one, despite his last two flops." Danica sipped her wine. "So… Michael is very proud of Jamie's movie deal and asked me for a little help."

Sarah leaned forward. "And?"

"Jamie just got a deal with a very prestigious director." Danica beamed like she'd done something to make it happen. "Michael thinks this movie will finally show the world what a great actor Jamie is. This is where you come in."

"I have absolutely no idea where you're going with this," Sarah said.

"Jamie has the starring role. He'll play a famous American baker who moves to France to open a patisserie." Danica winked at Sarah. "You get it now, right?"

"I can see how this movie might be good for him. But what does this have to do with me?"

"Well, you're a baker."

"Right."

Sarah tried not to show her frustration. She owed

Danica for getting her the hell out of San Francisco after she broke up with Robert, and for talking her into renting a room here. If she hadn't taken Danica's advice, she didn't know what her life would be like. She glanced over her shoulder at the villa. Decades of wear may have chipped away some of the mansion's original opulence, and the hundreds of acres that used to be Castelli vineyards had whittled away to just ten, but everything about the place seemed like the good dream she'd needed for a while.

Sarah turned to back Danica. "So I know how to bake, so what?"

"And you own the Vine Café." Danica's eyes sparkled. "And even though you serve breakfast and lunch, it's almost exactly like a patisserie."

"So?"

"Oh, just cut to the chase, Danica!" Juliet interrupted, bouncing from her chair and turning to Sarah. "Danica promised Michael you'd teach Jamie how to make pastry and let him work at the Vine Café. He starts tomorrow."

"What?" Sarah may have needed rescuing after the Robert debacle, but that didn't give Danica carte blanche to interfere with every aspect of her life, especially her new business. "What the hell did you do Danica? Whatever happened to asking my permission first?"

"I didn't promise anything, Sarah, so just calm down. I just told him it might be okay if Jamie came in tomorrow to meet you. It's not a big deal. Is eleven a good time?"

"What are you talking about? No!" Sarah ran her hands through her hair. "It's not a good time and neither is twelve, one or five. There is no good time to be training drama queens, or kings, or anyone, and you should know that."

"Consider the free publicity you'd get." Juliet looked hopeful. "I don't know if I can swing a morning show interview, but I'd mention a Jamie Santino sighting at your place. He's big."

"I haven't even been open a year." Sarah scooted back in her chair, wanting to get as far away from Danica's ridiculous idea as she could. "I'm just settling in. I'm not ready for any more anything."

"You are ready. It's time," Danica said. "It's time to wipe that rat bastard Robert completely off your plate, just like you wiped him off your pastry table."

Sarah put her glass down and stood up. Danica knew better than to mention his name. The past six months hadn't been easy, but she'd finally managed to create a new life in Sonoma without him. She still caught herself thinking about Robert and the future they'd planned, but his betrayal didn't haunt her as much as it had in the first few months. "I didn't wipe the pastry table. I sterilized it about fifty million times for your information and training some actor in my brand new business has nothing to do with Robert."

“Okay ladies, settle down.” Juliet reached for the bottle of Chardonnay. She stood and poured each another glass. “This is Chill Hour, remember?”

“This is what I get for helping.” Danica pouted.

It had been like throwing a dart for the first time and hitting the bull’s-eye for Sarah to score the lease for the Vine Café's sweet location on 1st Street East. She found it just a few months after moving here. The shop was smack dab in the heart of Sonoma, right across the street from all of the action at the Sonoma Plaza. The community gathered there for farmers markets in the summer, the Harvest Festival and the blessing of the grapes in the fall, and Santa visited every second week of December to light the city’s Christmas tree.

But Sarah wasn’t appreciating much of anything because she’d barely made it out of bed. She’d spent a brutal night deliberating every ‘What if?’ and ‘Why?’ of her new role of movie star mentor. When she’d finally fallen asleep, she'd slept face down, drooling on her pillow through her three-thirty alarm.

Sarah rummaged through the deep recesses of her bag in the dark, quiet alley for her keys.

"What the heck . . . I just had them in my hands," she said to the little orange tabby who always managed to appear at the side door of her café. She shook the purse harder until she heard a familiar muffled jingle and then pulled the keys out.

Sarah unlocked the door and stepped inside the kitchen with kitty following behind. Comforting smells and gleaming stainless counters welcomed her. She filled a ramekin with the organic cat food she'd finally succumbed to buying at The Granary, and placed it in the corner for the cat. She grabbed her apron from the closet, shoved her not quite dry hair in a net and got busy baking.

By ten, right on schedule, the serious crush of commuters and farmers left and a second wave of customers arrived. Every seat at the marble counter, salvaged from an old San Francisco Victorian, had someone sitting on it. The few coveted tables on the sidewalk and all five tables inside were full. The two takeout lines, one for pastries and one for coffee, were locked and loaded with customers.

Sarah buzzed, on rote, staying ahead of the orders side by side with Alicia, the part-time barista she'd just hired.

While counting the cups waiting on the counter for pickup Sarah yelled, “One double cap light foam, espresso, mocha light extra shot!” Pivoting back, she grabbed the next order.

“Double shot, caramel macchiato,” she said, ducking behind the espresso machine.

The entire room came to a standstill the second the little bell on the door rang, and he walked in, except Jamie Santino didn’t walk. Swaggering with a casual ease, he flung a look around the room before getting in Sarah’s line.

“You have got to be kidding me,” Sarah said under her breath, sneaking another glimpse of the Adonis patiently standing in line. Even though every woman scrambled to offer him a place in line in front of her, he declined and didn’t seem to mind waiting his turn. He caught her peeking, flashed a mischievous grin and gave her a little I-see-you wave.

Jamie Santino didn’t have to do anything to get attention. It was impossible not to look at him. The seated customers seemed to forget about their food and shifted in their seats, begging for a better look. Unless they’d been living in caves, they’d seen his face and other assorted attributes before, either on film, a billboard, a magazine cover or television.

His bare bottom was so delectable that movie

reviewers seeing it for the first time in *After the Lost* wanted to know if he'd used a stunt double. Headlines like "No Butts About It, It's His!" and "The Power of Perfection" graced many of the tabloids. Jamie finally advanced in line and stood directly in front of Sarah.

He shrugged a strand of sandy blond hair away from his green eyes and she locked onto his gaze. Staying behind the espresso maker for protection, Sarah barely found her voice, "May I help you?"

"Sure can," he said, his sparkling eyes not wavering.

Sarah gripped the coffee stained rag, hoping it would stabilize her.

He beckoned her with his index finger. "Could you come a little closer?"

He didn't need to ask. The total package of Jamie Santino, the way he looked, more mouthwatering than anything she'd ever even thought of baking, made her lean toward him without a second thought.

Bending over the counter close enough that Sarah felt his breath tickle her neck and with sex oozing from his voice, he rumbled in her ear, "I guess you're my boss now, baby. Your wish is my command."

She shot back behind the counter and took a deep breath. "Danica said you'd be coming in. You must be Mr. Santino." She flung out her hand to shake his in such an exaggerated way, she felt like an idiot, so she forced a smile to take it down a notch. “I’m Sarah Dupont, nice to meet you.”

Jamie didn’t take her hand. Instead, he stepped back and moved his gaze slowly up her arm, lingering at her neck and down to her breasts. He didn’t seem to mind that Sarah was watching. It felt like an hour had passed before he grasped her hand and gave it a firm squeeze, causing her body to surge on contact.

Stop. Stop this right now. He's only an actor. He's just a normal guy who has a GQ rating instead of an IQ; that's all. She tried not to look too anxious waiting for him to speak.

“Sarah,” he said looking like a lion licking his paws, “call me Jamie, darlin’.”

She nodded up and down. Yes. Yes, he is so very gorgeous.

“Do you want to get this party started?” he asked flashing his dimples.

Holy hell.

“Let me show you around.” Sarah handed her rag to Alicia, motioning for her to take over espresso duties and ran her hands over the front of her apron smoothing wrinkles that weren’t there. She made a mental note to kill Danica.

“The place isn’t very big, let’s start in the kitchen.” Sarah led the way, with Jamie close behind. She felt the sweat puddling under her armpits, and couldn't remember if she'd put deodorant on that morning. When she saw how much her hair had flattened and how pale she was in the mirror above the hamper in the kitchen, she freaked.

"This is where it all happens. Yup, right here in this kitchen." Sarah extended her arm dramatically, presenting the room like it was a dream vacation, and she was a game show host. She stunned herself again when she caught another glimpse of herself in the mirror and noticed two smudges of chocolate frosting in the two worst places possible on the front of her apron.

She shot for nonchalance and said to her staff, "This is Jamie Santino. He'll be helping us out for a little while." She held her chin up.

Instead of greeting or even offering Jamie a gesture of any kind, the crew just stood there like dented soup cans.

Great, just great, after all of the work she'd put into creating a comfortable workplace she'd have to survive two weeks of this?

Sarah nodded to Manny, who always knew how to break the ice. "Manny is my right hand, Jamie. You'll be able to learn a lot from him . . . Isn't that so, Manny?"

Manny adjusted his pose so he stood even straighter. He planted his feet, folded his arms in front of him and shrugged. “Whatever you say,” he said, without moving an inch.

Jamie observed him but said nothing.

“And this is our walk-in.” Sarah pointed to the massive refrigerator, thinking of her hairy legs shuffling toward it. “Go ahead, you can open it and take a peek.”

Jamie turned his back to her, opened the latch and bent over for a look inside. She tried to stop herself, but couldn’t resist checking out his buns.

“All righty then.” She sighed.

“So this will be okay?”

“What?"

“My working here?” Jamie asked.

“Sure, why not?” She sighed in resignation. “I think we can handle it for a few weeks.”

“Thank you,” he said, startling her with the most beautiful smile she’d ever seen. “What time do you want me?”

“Anytime.”

“Anytime?” Sparks flew from his eyes, and Jamie maintained a stare long enough to mesmerize her.

“Four a.m. I mean, if you want. I know it’s kind of early, but I usually get here around three forty-five, and I can show you how to make the most delicious shortbread cookies tomorrow.” She wanted to smack herself for babbling.

"I needed you to say yes today." He moved toward her, and Sarah gasped, simultaneously sucking in her stomach.

"Thank you so much." He took her hand in both of his, holding it for an instant. He started to leave and stopped. "I'll see you in the morning," he said, leveling her with the naughtiest grin.

Whatever switch that had been stuck on the off position for Sarah turned on.

Acknowledgments

My Love Train of thanks:

- To my incredible sisterhood of friends in Sonoma and Napa who fill me with love, wisdom, and gratitude every time I see them.
- To Vickie. Your love and encouragement will stay with me always.
- To my parents for making my Christmases magical.
- To Cindy Sue.
- To my family and constant writing companion Luciana Parmigiana.
- Many thanks to author Belinda Riehl.
- To Facebook, Instagram, Twitter followers and friends. So many of my days start with all of you.
- To the beautiful wine country town of St. Helena and to Bunny Foo Foo, the *real* sculpture that inspired this story.

And finally to my readers who make everything

Kate Kisset

possible!

May your days be merry and bright. xo

Playlist

Christmas season starts at our house the day after Thanksgiving. *If* I'm writing about Christmas, the festivities begin the moment I have the idea for the story. Even though I'm not on the radio in San Francisco anymore, music is still one of my greatest passions. My trusty Sony MDR-7506 headphones are never far from me. It's no surprise to anyone who knows me that I would write a song about a singer. I'm in love with Trace Montgomery. :-)

In *Kissing Mr. Mistletoe*, several songs became part of Monique and Trace's story and are mentioned by name. Country star Trace Montgomery, the main character of *Kissing Mr. Mistletoe* even makes up his own words to "Winter Wonderland."

If *Kissing Mr. Mistletoe* were a soundtrack, from start to finish, in order, here's how it would sound to me.

"Blame it On The Mistletoe" —Toby Keith
"Baby, It's Cold Outside" (feat. Meghan Trainor)—Brett Eldredge Meghan Trainor
"Winter Wonderland" —Ella Fitzgerald
"All I Want For Christmas is You" —Lady

Antebellum
"I'll Be Home for Christmas" —Brad Paisley
"It Won't Be Christmas Without You" —Brooks & Dunn
"Run Rudolph Run" —Chuck Berry
"Something About December" —Christina Perri
"The Christmas Song" —Vince Guaraldi Trio
"Please Come Home For Christmas" —Kelly Clarkson
"A Holly Jolly Christmas" —Burl Ives
"Have Yourself A Merry Little Christmas" —Lady Antebellum
"What Are You Doing New Year's Eve?" —Harry Connick Jr.

About the Author

Former San Francisco radio disc jockey Kate Kisset has a passion for telling great stories. After playing thousands of pop, country, rock and oldies tunes for her primarily female fan base, she changed her tune and became an author.

Kissing Mr. Mistletoe is the first novella in her *Holiday in the Vineyards* series.

She lives in Northern California and Santa Barbara with her family and rescue pup "editor" Luciana Parmigiana, where she hikes, reads, listens to music, and drinks wine.

For exclusive updates, including story excerpts, books, and secrets from wine country, reach out to Kate:

Visit Kate's website at: http://www.katekisset.com

Made in the USA
Middletown, DE
09 December 2016